Praise for *In a Veil of Mist*

"A moving portrait of a place and its people … a quiet, sad but brilliant novel." ANTONIA SENIOR, BOOK OF THE MONTH, *TIMES*

"Shows yet again how a good novel is capable of making you think and feel at the same time … a rich and sympathetic portrayal of island life in all its diversity … timely and compelling … a novel to savour." ALLAN MASSIE, *SCOTSMAN*

"Set in [Murray's] native Lewis as firmly as the stones at Callanish … it is so credibly drawn that the book is almost a ticket to the island … it seems an even more impressive achievement than ever." DAVID ROBINSON, *BOOKS FROM SCOTLAND*

"Human and relatable … beautifully depicting life in the Outer Hebrides. A gripping, intelligent and often humorous read." *SCOTTISH FIELD*

"A well-written and well-crafted novel from an author at the height of his powers." ERIC MACINTYRE, *OBAN TIMES*

"Where the book really scores is in Murray's familiarity with … [the island] culture … a living community of varied characters with generations of history behind them, giving his story depth and solidity." *HERALD*

"A wonderfully evocative book … brought to the page … with consummate skill … We'd strongly recommend [it to] anyone looking for really strong and memorable fiction about Scotland … outstanding." *UNDISCOVERED SCOTLAND*

Praise for *As the Women Lay Dreaming*

WINNER: PAUL TORDAY MEMORIAL PRIZE 2020

SHORTLISTED: AUTHOR'S CLUB BEST FIRST NOVEL AWARD 2019 *an* HERALD SCOTTISH CULTURE LITERATURE AWARD 2019

LONGLISTED: HIGHLAND BOOK PRIZE 2018 *and* HISTORICAL WRITERS' ASSOCATION DEBUT CROWN 2019

WALTER SCOTT PRIZE "ACADEMY RECOMMENDS" LISTED

/ con

"A powerful novel … A poignant exploration of love, loss and survivor's guilt." NICK RENNISON, SUNDAY TIMES

"Beauty, poetry and heart … a brilliant blend of fact and fiction, full of memorable images and singing lines of prose." SARAH WATERS

"A searing, poetic meditation on stoicism and loss." MARIELLA FROSTRUP, BBC RADIO 4 OPEN BOOK

"A classic *Bildungsroman* … A work of imagination which reads like experienced truth. It's the kind of book … that can enrich your life." ALLAN MASSIE, SCOTSMAN, BEST BOOKS OF 2018

"An evocative painter of landscapes and a deeply sympathetic writer … a space for forgotten voices to sound." STEPHANIE CROSS, DAILY MAIL

"An assured journey through trauma, love and loss." HERALD

"I loved this book." DOUGLAS STUART, BOOKER PRIZE–WINNING AUTHOR OF SHUGGIE BAIN

"A poignant novel." NICOLA STURGEON

"Beautifully and sensitively told, by one of the great lyrical writers of our time." CATHY MACDONALD

"A powerful book … moving and beautiful." SCOTS WHAY HAE

Praise for Donald S Murray's previous books
"Deeply moving." Will Self, DAILY TELEGRAPH

"The story is told with great charm, and tinged with a spirit of loss and yearning." Philip Marsden, SPECTATOR

"A gregarious and engaging raconteur." ECONOMIST

In a Veil
of Mist

Donald S Murray

Saraband

Published by Saraband
3 Clairmont Gardens
Glasgow, G3 7LW
Scotland, UK

www.saraband.net

ISBN: 9781913393007

1 3 5 7 9 10 8 6 4 2

*A note on the use of Gaelic: Some traditional song lyrics and
sayings are written with spellings that may have been superseded by
today's conventions. The author has made spelling choices to balance
authenticity to the period with current standard Gaelic.*

*This is a work of fiction, even though it is based on a true incident in history.
All characters and events are a result of the author's imagination except
where mentioned in the author's note at the end of the text.*

To Maggie with love.

Sometimes death sweeps in like an eagle
employing beak and talons to make its savage kill.
At other times, its slow approach will start
with a trembling of fingers, a startle of the heart.
Sometimes its coming's foreshadowed by a howl
not unlike a wolf's, a low-pitched growl
accompanying the bite and grip of pain.
Or it might go unnoticed; a trail of mist
descending on a landscape, clouding vision like a fist
clenching; an unexpected fall of rain.

To the memory of Murdo Macfarlane (1901–1982), John
'Hoddan' Macdonald (1925–2007) and all those others
who gave my people the chance to sing.

Part One

Beum

- beat

Òran Cladaich

Greas, greasaibh a dhìreadh
muir chan fhuirich rinn.
Seo reothart 'Ill'Bhride,
'n tìde builichibh.

The Shoreline Song

Rouse yourself, climb quickly,
the sea will not stay still.
This is the springtide of the oystercatcher,
the hour for us to stir.

By Murdo Macfarlane – Murchadh MacPhàrlain

1

John wasn't sure what made him so clumsy these days – the roll of the sea, the absurd nature of his clothes or the thoughts about Lillian that crowded his head most of the time.

Boom! And she was in there, drinking perhaps, in the Hermitage or the Lime View, with some dark-haired stranger he'd never come across before. The man's features were always blurred and hard to distinguish, the shadow of a nightmare that might only exist in John's head. She, however, looked real and convincing, though different every time he pictured her, as if she was trying on every item of clothing in her wardrobe. Sometimes, a red scarf coiled around her neck. Red shoes danced upon her feet. Scarlet lipstick daubed her mouth as she sang along to one of the Nat King Cole songs she loved, unaware of the irony of the words. (*Unforgettable…*) At other times, she wore the dark blue overcoat he'd bought, the one she had insisted on him getting for her, even though he tried to tell her they couldn't afford it. They were that short of money at the time. Her long, black hair hung loose upon her shoulders. A cigarette dangled from her fingers. She wore a knitted, pale blue dress. She petted a neighbour's dog, bending over to tousle its fur. Her features were so clear to him at moments like these that he could even imagine the words she was saying.

'Oh, John Herrod! He's nothing to me. Just a big, clumsy oaf who I made the mistake of marrying.'

He tried his best to focus on where he was at that moment. The miles of hostile, barren moor. The fringe of sand in the distance. The dark faces of cliffs. Croft-houses. Crops of potatoes, turnips, oats. And the tight stretch of the Minch, its dark surface split and splintered by the wind. Waves swathed the deck of the *Ben Lomond*, their spume resembling the veil that Lillian had worn only a year before, and the wedding dress, too, she had on that day. Each time a wave swept over either him or the deck below his feet, he shivered, the shock of its impact reminding him of the coldness she had displayed towards him the last time he was home on leave, how she turned away again and again in their bed.

'No chance... No possibility... I'm not in the mood...'

He grimaced, wishing he was somewhere else at moments like these, somewhere he might find reassurance, an opportunity to convince himself that his new wife wasn't spending much of her life in another man's arms. It was something his mother had warned him about.

'She's not ready for settling down. Far too young. Far too restless. You'll rue the day.'

He had shaken his head, sure that she was misjudging Lillian, believing that his mother would come to the same conclusion no matter which woman he might choose to share his life.

'You're wrong, Mum. Give it a while. You'll get to trust her.'

Yet his mother had been right. He knew that now, for all he tried to chase the thought from his head. Despite all his efforts, the truth of her words kept penetrating, seeping through the armour of the white protective suit – complete with goggles and respirator – that he wore most days. His doubts and suspicions distracted him as he worked, hauling the transit boxes into the animal store in the vessel's hold. His fingers kept slipping, his concentration faltering from time to time. Sometimes his shoulders brushed against others working on the boat, knocking a box from another man's grasp.

'Herrod! What the hell's up with you?'

He had no answer. How on earth could he tell any of these men about what he thought might be happening back home? And even if he did, what the hell could they do about it? Besides, he knew that some of them suffered from a mood that was as dark and distracted as his own. It was the nature of the work that was getting to them: all that shifting of boxes filled with guinea pigs and monkeys from the 'clean' to 'dirty' rooms; hauling cages to the pontoon that was fixed a short distance away in the seas below Cellar Head on the island. Afterwards, there would be the burning of those animals that had survived the swathe of gas – a flame flickering on the deck, a column of dark smoke rising. The guinea pigs chirruping, fighting off the grip of gloved hands, tussling with the strength of their custodians. The monkeys agitated and angry, as if they were people complaining about their lot, and sometimes sinking their teeth into the human fingers that hauled them in and out of the cages, drawing blood. The monkeys bit them in other ways, their presence down below forcing the men to ask questions of themselves, like why the hell they were here tormenting these poor creatures with gases and sprays.

The officers all had answers, of course. They talked about Korea endlessly, how the Americans had bombed Pyongyang and some hydroelectric dams in the North over the last while, how the likes of McCarthy in the States might be right, that Churchill and his kind were too weak in the way they dealt with the Soviets. Perhaps it was time they took more drastic action: an atom bomb or two, some of the gases they were testing here. It was the only way to treat Stalin and his kind. After all, it had brought one war to a sudden end – why not use it to stop the Reds winning this one?

'Show a little teeth,' Shepherd would say. He was the biologist in charge of the project, who would underline his boldness by declaring, 'It's the only way to get respect from that crowd.'

But John and a number of others only had uncertainties. Some of them – like his fellow Liverpudlian, Lambert – would whisper their grievances from time to time, mourning the dead monkeys they gathered up on the pontoon after the white trail of gas had passed. The two of them stood on it a short time, noting how it sloped in the water.

'Do you know what I feel like here, Herrod?' Lambert said. 'One of the three wise monkeys myself. See no evil, hear no evil, speak no bloody evil. And yet it's all around me at the moment – that's all I touch and feel and smell. The rancid stink of downright wickedness. There's no God or angel that can defend what we're doing here. Not even Christ Himself.'

John shook his head, preferring not to think about it. Just now he only had one true vision of wickedness. He saw her sometimes instead of the monkeys, that red scarf she wore tight around her throat, that lipstick a slash of blood across her mouth. He would shudder each time he thought about this, knowing that in his rage he was capable of doing something terrible, that he could perform the act with greater force and conviction even than these American pilots who flew daily over North Korea, dropping bombs on those who lived in the villages and townships below their wings.

2

It was the dead fish she noticed first. The silvery skin of ling. A clutch of coalfish tangled among seaweed. Other fish stranded on the sand. Too many to be normal or natural. Jessie had stood there for ages watching them, bemused at their arrival on the shore. And then there was the day a couple of seals were washed up, stretched out on the edge of the tide, their flesh squabbled over by gulls, torn and shredded. She had never seen anything quite like it in all the years she had stepped on either Garry Beach or the Tràigh Mhòr, looking for flotsam the Minch had washed up on the tide. Things like nets swept from the deck of a fishing boat, a shattered tree trunk that might have floated in their direction from one of the rivers in the Highlands, even once a thick *geansaidh*, stripped, perhaps, from a fisherman's back. These gifts from the sea were always useful. A net could be draped over the top of a haystack. Timber might be used for a roof or even to weigh down a stack of oats or hay. A *geansaidh* could be washed and mended, given to one of the many bachelors in the village. They were always in need of clothes and they sometimes had no women in their lives to help provide them. A few hours and the click of knitting needles at the fireside and a quick repair could be done, clothing provided that would keep them warm in the winter.

But the fish and seals were strange: the fact that they had

shoaled up dead on the beach in such numbers. The way, too, there hadn't been a storm a night or two before, as there so often was on this edge of coastline, bringing all sorts of arrivals to the coast.

Yet odder still was what Jessie encountered a day or two later. She saw it from a distance – on the border of sea and sand – shifting back and forth on the tide, as if it was breathing. It looked like a dirty rag of cloud that had been toppled to earth, though more solid and substantial than that. Like the mound of seals and fish the other day, the gulls were sweeping down to feed on it, calling out and tearing at it with their beaks. She made her way towards the heap, tightening her scarf against the chill of the wind, bracing herself against its force, gasping as she came closer to what the sea had left on the beach. She stepped forward tentatively towards the pile, walking past the cattle grazing on the machair's edge. It looked as if a clutch of small animals were spread out on the sand, all beasts unknown to her. They weren't cats and dogs, the creatures that the local crofters often drowned in the sea in these parts – when too many kittens had been born, when a collie had turned on someone or grown too old to round up sheep. Their presence would have no effect on her whatsoever. Far too familiar. No. This was different. Some of these creatures had white fur and small, beady eyes – those that hadn't had their sight plucked by beaks, that is. They had expressions similar to those of children who had just been born. Others were like rats, but fat and round, as if they had been over-fed. She had never seen either of them before. She shivered when she saw them, tugging tighter her old tweed coat. There was something that disgusted her about the sight, something that wasn't real or natural.

Jessie wondered how they had reached here, what time or tide had brought them this way. For a moment, she wondered if they had anything to do with the vessel, the *Ben Lomond*, which had been anchored in the Minch, south of the Tràigh Mhòr, not far from Tolsta Head, over the last week or so. Some of her neighbours had said there was something strange about it. It was a large grey boat, a converted tank-landing ship, bulky and oppressive, and then there were these motor boats that kept going back and forth to it, sometimes towards Stornoway, at other times towards some kind of platform that was a short distance away, those on board moving boxes to and fro. Sometimes they even hoisted the motor boats up the side of the vessel. This happened each time the waves grew high and choppy, when the wind rose up.

And some neighbours had seen the red warning flag being raised, a veil of white smoke rising from the pontoon's deck a few moments later. It trailed across its surface like sea-spray but more persistent and long lasting, misting the crest of waves. Some of the local boats ignored the signal. Pretending not to see the flag, they just carried on fishing. Domhnall Iain, a former fisherman and one of the village's older men, said it resembled the gas that had cloaked his trench when he fought in the Great War. Others laughed at him behind his back for that, dismissing his words.

'*B' eòlach do sheanair air.* Nonsense. He's never quite escaped from Flanders. His mind still goes back there from time to time.'

They were always like that, ignoring what they didn't believe or hadn't experienced. They were especially like that with Jessie, never quite forgetting the episode she had gone through back in the 1920s, when she was barely out of her teens. George had never written to her from Canada or the States, wherever he now was – if, indeed, he lived anywhere at all. One time she had walked across the moor to the other side of the island, visiting one of her relatives, Catriona, who lived with her husband, Tormod, in the village of South Dell. Jessie had the strange notion she could call across the Atlantic to George from that shoreline, standing, perhaps, in the shade of the lighthouse that was a few miles away from their home, relying on the flash of its light to beckon him back to Tolsta. Or even use the foghorn she had heard about, summoning him with its deep, sonorous notes.

It was Catriona who, over the passing years, had convinced Jessie there were other methods she could employ to bring her man back home. Clasping hands and closing eyes, her cousin had uttered one of those loud prayers for which she was known. Some said Catriona did this so that her words could reach the house of her former father-in-law in Tolsta, part of the family who had raised her son, Roderick, after her first husband had drowned, falling from the deck of a fishing boat, his feet tangled in a net.

'Oh, Lord, take care of Your servant Jessie here. Teach her that there are other ways in which her words can reach the man she wishes to marry, who lives so far away from here now in the New World, where he stays. Teach her to speak instead to You so that Thou might listen, pass on the hopes and dreams, the urgency and desperation of her prayers to the one she loves. Let us hope, that if he is so disposed, he might listen and return here to these shores or – if not – send her the means to make her own way across the seas to America. And if not, if there is no future for her and this man, teach her to be content with this, to accept the wisdom of Thy will, in the hope and trust she can find peace and contentment.'

And Catriona had taken her home across the moor, near the shoulder of Beinn Dail, lochs and streams that were nameless to Jessie, unfamiliar patches of green bog. Her companion, however, had not taken her all the way to Tolsta. Shaking and trembling, Catriona had stood a half-mile away from the village edge, knowing that all around her was familiar – the edge of Loch Mor Shanndabhat, the beginnings of the Garry River – and she could find her way home. It was as if she was terrified of the sense of loss that might overwhelm her if she stepped any closer, glimpsed the boy she had been forced to surrender all those years before.

'*Siuthad. Siuthad.* You go on your way now. I don't need to go any farther than this.'

Jessie, too, had hesitated before going towards her home, aware that people would be talking, mentioning those hours of delusion she had suffered, the belief that she could call across the Atlantic from the shoreline of South Dell. She could imagine some of the village youngsters mocking and imitating her, standing on a pinnacle of rock and yelling towards the sea.

'Oh, George! George! Seoras! Seoras! Can you hear me?'

Or they might stand on the bridge that Leverhulme built in the twenties, the one they all said led to nowhere, part of a road that was planned to take people all the way to Ness, passing Caisteal a' Mhorair with its fallen, toppled stones, the shielings at Dìobadal, Filiscleitir, Cladach Chuidhsiadar, all the empty places that had at one time rippled with the voices of people.

'Oh, George! Come back to me!'

She had taken a long time to regain the trust of people after that, always conscious of the barely suppressed shrug when she spoke, the raising of an eyebrow, the look of dismissal in their eyes. 'Oh, she's becoming strange again. It's happening once more.' She did not want to go through the likes of that. No. She had to have proof that she had seen these creatures on the beach. Otherwise they would think she was going mad.

It was for this reason that she took off her headscarf, using it to wrap around one of the tiny creatures that had landed on the beach. An animal that looked almost human, with arms and legs, a tiny human head, a furry body and a tail. She walked home, taking the bundle with her. She would show it to those who lived around her, a dumb witness to the fact that she wasn't – once again – going mad.

* * *

'It's a monkey. I saw some of these when I was in Gibraltar. They called them Barbary apes there,' Duncan declared when he stopped his bus to speak with Jessie, who was walking along the road with her bundle in her hands. 'Never thought I'd see them in my life again. Where did you come across one?'

Jessie gabbled out her story to the broad-shouldered bus-driver with his black, combed back hair, bright blue eyes and red cheeks. As ever, he was wearing his neatly pressed jacket and trousers, the reason why – according to some in the village – he had never had a girlfriend. ('Too scared of getting crumpled,' they declared.) She told him how she had come across this creature, along with others, on the beach. There was something else there, too, some other animal she had left on the sand, not lifting it up.

'Let's go down and see what it is.'

'But your bus... You have to go to Stornoway.'

'Och, I've got time. Plenty of time.'

'You will be late.'

'Away,' he said, grinning at her. 'I've been that a few times before.'

'All right then,' she laughed. 'I'm glad you'll be there.'

Duncan took an empty sack from the bus with him as they headed down the croft. One that had been used for turnips or potatoes before. 'For the creatures. Whatever they are,' he explained.

All the time he went in the direction of the shore, he was talking, his face more flushed than usual, eyes glinting, mouth twisting with the weight of words. He was speaking of things Jessie had never heard from his lips before. He had always been quiet in her company, but now he was talking endlessly, telling of how he had spent some of his war years in Gibraltar, helping to dig out the tunnels that had been hewn into the Rock for the protection of the troops stationed at the narrow entrance to the Mediterranean that the garrison overlooked.

'It was really hard work. But it needed to be done. We had to keep control of the place. Otherwise the Nazis and their friends would have control of the entire Mediterranean, Malta, North Africa, Egypt. It was because of that the Italians kept bombing us. Night after night. Day after day. You couldn't get a moment's sleep or rest. People being killed. Yet all that seemed to worry our officers were the bloody monkeys. There were only a few of them left when I first arrived. Only a handful. And that apparently mattered. There was some story that they appeared to believe in. A wee bit like the tales your father used to tell.'

Jessie smiled at that, recalling how her father always used to relate stories to her and the neighbours' children; tales of the legendary island murderer Mac an t-Stronaich, the seal people, the blue men of the Minch, how certain wells were sacred and cured those who brought its water to their lips. 'The blue men of the Minch,' she could remember him saying, his face taking on something of the sheen of the blaze before him, 'they were dark-skinned people who swam between the islands and the mainland. They could sink boats if you failed to greet them, answering their words in verse.' And then there would be the inevitable look from her mother. She had been brought up a Free Presbyterian and didn't really approve of such tales. 'Alasdair,' she might say, 'why are you encouraging such nonsense?'

'What was the legend about the monkeys?' Jessie asked Duncan.

'Oh, if the creatures ever disappeared, Gibraltar would be lost to the British. Spain would take it over once again. And that's why Churchill and all the high heid-yins decided that they'd have to bring more to the Rock after they started disappearing. Sent out a boat to Africa to take more back to Gibraltar. I remember the poor creatures chattering when they came to shore, no doubt as confused as we were about what was happening to them. Just like this fellow you found must have been.'

'Aye.'

She looked out at the croftland that surrounded them. The fields of oats that were beginning to turn green. The odd acre of turnips, also beginning to show their leaves. The birds singing. The calls of starlings, pigeons, sparrows unspooling among the grass. Though the summer had not yet arrived with its warmth, she could feel it coming, its presence at the verges of their lives. The seasons shifting in the soil and wind. Even within her own flesh and bones. For all that she wanted to leave the place with George some three decades or so before, it was all she had ever known – the waters of the Minch confining her, the windows of the houses looking out at her every move, even this quick, brisk walk she was embarking on with Duncan down to the Tràigh Mhòr. She knew that there were some among the older men of the village whose gaze still followed her movements, noting how her body was still slim and strong; how, for all the grey frost that had settled on her hair, her face was still unlined, her eyes continuing to dance and sparkle. There would be heads clicking with thought as they followed her progress today, wondering what she was doing with a robust, strong bachelor quite a good few years younger than her. There would be some – like her neighbour, Mairead – who might even ask the question.

'What kind of monkey business were you up to down there?'

'None,' she would say before revealing the strange beast in her fingers.

'What on earth have you got there?' Mairead could ask when she saw the bundle, her nose twitching and troubling her face.

But with Duncan, there was nothing like that. He would talk to people in a different way from most around here. He spent much of his time in Stornoway, going to the Italian Lido Café with others from around the island or leafing through the newspapers in the Town Hall library, finding out what was happening in the world beyond North Tolsta. He was the one that told them all last February that the King had died, that his daughter Elizabeth was in Kenya when she heard the news that her father had passed away. He had informed those who travelled back and forth to Stornoway on his bus that the East Germans had their own army, and that Churchill had announced Britain now had an atomic bomb. ('Let's hope that Winston uses it,' one of the Church elders had said. 'There's a better chance of that happening now that Clem has gone.') Being a bus driver, he was a more effective bearer of news than those in the village with a wireless in their homes, for he could also tell them how so-and-so had passed away in, say, the nearby villages of Gress or Back or Tong, or exiled in Ness, Carloway or somewhere even further afield.

He was careful, too, about other matters, making sure at all times that his speech was sure and accurate, containing no falsehood or lie. It was why Jessie was glad he was alongside her when they stood among the marram grass and looked down towards the Tràigh Mhòr that day, seeing the men in their white suits in the exact place where she had found the corpses of the animals, lifting them with gloved fingers and placing them in sacks.

'You see what's happening?' She turned in Duncan's direction.

'Aye. I do.'

It was as if they were ghosts draped in white sheets, she thought to herself, gathering up the spirits of the dead.

3

Before running into Jessie and her bundle that day, Duncan's last few miles back to Tolsta – through Gress and Gleann Mhor – had been an interesting journey. He had spoken to Angus Murray, a slim, dark-skinned young man of his own age from Ness who was on his way to visit his relatives in Tolsta. ('I'll never hear the end of it if I don't go,' he had grinned. 'And at least this bus is a lot easier than what we used to do: trekking across the moorland.') On their way, they had swapped wars – Angus speaking about how he had spent much of the conflict on a minesweeper in Nicaragua and then Sierra Leone. The Nessman had tapped his wrist to show a brass watch he had obtained during his time in Central America.

'And in Sierra Leone?' Duncan asked. 'Did you get any souvenirs from there?'

'Just a dose of malaria,' Angus laughed. 'Still suffer from it occasionally, the way it hangs around. And a local tribe put on a special dance for me. For my twenty-first birthday. That was something I'll never quite forget.' The Nessman grinned. 'What about you? How did you ever end up in Gibraltar, of all places?'

'By accident,' Duncan replied. 'I said I was good at driving lorries. "Oh," they said, "that could be valuable. Do you fancy working with the Black Watch in Gibraltar? They're looking for lorry drivers down there. And as someone who comes from an island, you shouldn't feel too trapped there. Not like some of those we send. What do you think, eh?" And so I swapped one kind of rock for another. Lewisian gneiss for limestone.'

'An interesting exchange.'

'Aye. They didn't tell me the whole story. That I would get bombed a few times more often there than in Tolsta.'

'No doubt about that.'

He said goodbye to Angus, his last remaining passenger. A moment or two later, he saw Jessie.

Duncan normally grinned whenever he came across her. For a woman nearing the age of fifty, she was incredibly fit and nimble, even attractive if you ignored her collection of odd habits and eccentricities. But, most of all, it was these he noticed. She would invariably be carrying something she had picked up on her travels. Some afternoons she might be wheeling a load of seaweed for fertilising her crop of potatoes. At other times, she could be straining to carry a sack of winkles or even some plants that grew in the moor not far from Long Langabhat or among the bracken near Caisteal a' Mhorair. She'd search a stretch of sand for the red fronds of carrageen, making dessert from her finds. It was even said she sometimes collected the leaves from nettles on the edge of croftland, using this instead of tea from the local shop.

'She's the only one in these parts who doesn't rely on Dr Gillies or MacAulay for their medicine these days,' one of his passengers might say. 'Relies on her own efforts for cures.'

And then he'd smile when he saw the stuff she had gathered around her home at the southern end of the village. There were pieces of driftwood, sea-worn and shaped by waves; a stack of broken lobster creels; brightly coloured glass floats;

a few tattered and torn pieces of fishing net; a fish-box from Fraserburgh, that legend on its side calling for its return. Even an old broomstick, which had been washed up on the Tràigh Mhòr a couple of months before.

'Looks like it belongs to a witch,' he had joked with her after they had taken the dead monkey to the byre. 'Even if it is a very friendly one.'

'We people have to live up to our reputations,' she said, grinning.

But, that moment aside, this time he had left her with a stern and brooding expression on his face. The monkey – and his talk with Angus – had made him think both of his own war and those that had affected others in the village. As a child, he had only heard whispers about the Great War, how his mother had been in tears after her brother had been killed in the Dardanelles. Talk, too, of those lost in battles at land and sea. Those drowned the day of the *Iolaire*, the moment that had brought great sadness to the village with the loss of eleven men from within its boundaries.

He was also thinking of all he'd read the last while in the library, the newspapers he'd cast his eyes upon – how another war threatened and seemed likely. The fighting in Korea. A Swedish plane brought down by the Soviets. The nuclear tests the Yanks were undertaking in Nevada. (Operation Tumble-Snapper, they apparently called that one, following Operation Buster-Jangle before.) It looked as if another conflict was on its way, one that would be even more devastating and destructive than those that had gone before.

It might leave much of the world looking like the moor between Tolsta and Ness in the damp and desolate days of winter: not a sign of life upon it, apart from, perhaps, a crow picking the flesh from a sheep that lay dead beside an old shieling, the remnants of its walls the only evidence that human life had ever existed here on this island – and even then only briefly, at the height of summer. Or like the sands at the Tràigh Mhòr with only the whisper of waves as the tide delivered death to the shoreline, bringing the carcass of a whale or dolphin for gulls to devour…

He shook his head at the vision of it, imagining these acres he was driving by empty of the sheep that flocked within its grass, the rocks at the shoreline still and empty of fulmars, gannets, gulls.

Then there was the recollection of his own war days, when he'd driven the high, twisting roads of Gibraltar, up to the heights of the Moorish Castle, down to the lighthouse at Europa Point, delivering supplies to the men of the Black Watch tunnelling the rock. Those troops from Arbroath, Broughty Ferry, Montrose and Arbroath were hewing out their own versions of the Caledonian Canal, Fort William and Fort George within its vastness, spilling boulders and rubble down below from the place they called Jock's Balcony for lorry-drivers like him to lift and carry, dumping their loads down on the shoreline to extend the harbour. Within that huge bright and shining hulk of limestone, there were quarters for the men, laboratories, even a hospital with wards and operating theatres – an unimaginable warren of rooms. And all the time he drove up and down its slopes, he was aware that one false turn and his lorry could end up swerving into a stone wall or building, plummeting from the heights. He couldn't even pound his horn if someone stepped in front of his wheels.

Forbidden by the officers to make any noise or disturb the people living all around, he had to just clap his hand on the outside of the window or door on the driver's side.

There was the time, too, when he had been near South Barrack Square when a bomb dropped. He had stopped driving for a while after that, shuddering and shaking while he listened to the bark of the Rock guns, the boom of those on the Fleet. It had taken ages for him to get back into his lorry again, to resume his progress up the road to Princess Caroline's Battery. The shifting of gears seemed to set up a trembling in his own bones. What if he had been a hundred yards further down the road? What if he had been driving a little more slowly?

It was the thought of this that actually made the drive around the edge of the Gleann Mhor, just outside Tolsta, relaxed for him, for all that those who came from the island said it was one of the tightest and narrowest roads within its shores. The only thing that made him squeeze his foot on the brake was the prospect of a sheep rushing out before him, or the doctor's car coming towards him from the other direction. There was no enemy plane winging its way before him. No road giving way below his wheels.

Yet, because of the monkey he had seen wrapped up in Jessie's arms, the war had come back to him. Even that humiliating moment in his life when he was persuaded by the others in the garrison to visit the prostitutes in La Línea. ('Go on, teuchter laddie. Gi'e it yer best shot.') There was also the dead and wounded he had seen, the buildings destroyed, all brought into even more vivid focus in his mind when he drove past the cemetery in Gress. There were so many headstones. So many killed in conflict lying there.

He also saw the war's legacy in the passengers he picked up, so many still marked by their experiences during those years. There were men like George MacKay, or Seoras a'Cheic, who had been on the *Kingston Sapphire* with some of his fellow islanders in October 1940 when it was sunk by an Italian submarine. There were twenty-eight of them in the lifeboat, crammed there for fifteen days, till they were taken to Huelva in south-west Spain, not that far from him in Gibraltar, by the men working on a Spanish trawler.

'Our captain told us to strip and tear off every sign that we were part of the Navy. They thought we were fishermen just like themselves.'

Sometimes, however, the experience of conflict was still alive in their eyes: old Uisdean, whose gaze was always frantic and nervous, a legacy from his time at the Somme; Morag, from Back, whose husband had been drowned in the Battle of Jutland when the *Galatea* had gone down. Sometimes, it could be seen in their bodies. There was Seoras, from Lighthill, who lost his hand in an accident near Scapa Flow. And Finlay, from Tong, who had been wounded at Dunkirk. He had been crippled during his time there. Duncan would get out of his seat to help him board the bus.

'Och… That's so kind of you. So, so kind.'

Once Duncan had taken his seat again, he would smile to himself as he watched Finlay undertake his next move. Taking out a packet of Senior Service from his pocket, the man would light a cigarette, invariably borrowing someone else's box of matches to do so. Smoke swirled around in every direction as Finlay talked to his neighbours, asking how the fishing boats tied up at Port Chuil were doing. Aware that there was a chance he would be a passenger today, someone might have noticed what was happening there, brought a report to the traveller of all that was happening.

'There were six open boats lying there for the *lion beag* fishing,' Finlay might be told.

'Oh. That's good. That's good. So kind of you to notice that. So, so kind.'

As he drove, Duncan tried not to think about the dead creatures on the beach, concentrating instead on taking the long, slow curve out of Tong, passing, too, the tinker children as they played outside their tents at Blackwater. There were so few young men living in the community at the moment. Some of them were away building the hydro dams being constructed all across the Highlands over the last few years. Others were at the whaling in South Georgia or in the Merchant Navy. And then there were those who were undergoing National Service, preparing, perhaps, for the next war that was coming, fighting the Red Army across the bombed streets of Berlin. He shook his head again, trying to clear an image from his own past that had loomed up in his mind. It was of searchlights crossing the night sky over Gibraltar – like a tangle of barbed wire, a fishing net, complete with hooks, draped around darkness. Despite what had happened earlier, his thoughts didn't have to be about war and conflict. Why the hell should he think about that these days?

He didn't have to. He could think instead of Ina, the girl from James Mackenzie's tweed mill whom he often saw in the Lido. He would look at her fair hair, shy and reticent manner, the way she would cross her legs back and forth below the tweed skirt she had made for herself from a leftover piece of cloth. He wondered what made her so hard to talk to. Why was he unable to tell her exactly what was in his mind? He had tried to gather together his thoughts to ask her out on a few occasions, but somehow, the words slipped from him, dying on his tongue.

4

'You were spotted down there,' Shepherd said.

'We were?'

'Yes. We kept our binoculars on you all the time you were out there. A couple were watching you. A man and woman. Two of the locals. Noting all you were doing.'

'Sorry, sir.'

'It just goes to show the consequences of mistakes, how things can go wrong even when you try to set them right. One reason why these mistakes should be avoided in the first place.'

'Yes, sir.'

Shepherd stared in the direction of the three men that were in front of him. A tall, broad-shouldered man with sharp blue eyes, an unlined face and thick, grey, brushed back hair, there always seemed to be a discrepancy between his youthful looks and the stern, commanding way he spoke. Even the sharpness of his intelligence didn't help. He was one of those people incapable of relaxing with anyone on board. Unlike some of the others who held positions of authority, he never forgot his role for a moment. It was as if he emerged from his bunk every morning with his shirt and tie in place, his white coat uncreased and buttoned.

'And even when or if they've been made, you should always keep an eye out in case someone might be watching you. That's what you lot failed to do there. Failed to be vigilant at all times.

Failed to be aware.'

'Yes, sir.'

'Sorry, sir.'

'It reminds me of the last time we were this far north. Some ten years ago or so. Testing out anthrax spores on Gruinard Island near Aultbea, not far from Loch Ewe where the Arctic Convoy were holed up. We thought we had limited the spread of the spores to the island's shores. And then, guess what, Herrod?'

'Mistakes were made, sir.' John had heard Shepherd come out with the spiel before. For all that he was a knowledgeable and talented scientist, there were limits to the variety of either his information or words. There were occasions when he recited the facts about his time in Gruinard: '*We estimated that all animals and human beings within a range of 200 yards of the explosion of our bomblets would be infected and die. Those within 400 yards of the release of the aerosol particle would be at serious risk of fatal infection. Along with wind direction and proximity to the mainland, it's the reason why we can't use that island anymore. We were lucky getting off so lightly the first time.*'

They had heard his justification for what they were doing here a thousand times. It was different to what other officers said – as if he had wrestled with the nature of their work, trying to explain it to himself, make a case for his actions if he ever ended up in the dock: '*Some people don't understand the importance of all we're doing here. They find it reprehensible, disgusting, unacceptable. They don't appear to comprehend how it might be necessary for the survival of this country. It would help protect us if the Soviets ever used biological weapons on us:*

to know how to react to them, predict even what direction they will travel, how weather – sunlight or cloud – might affect their progress. We need to know these things before a plague is visited on us, to discover what, exactly, we should do.'

Shepherd tapped his fingers on the table before he started to speak, nodding his head. 'Exactly that, Herrod. Mistakes were made. There were some dead sheep and cattle in the crofts neighbouring the island. A few dead sheep washed onto the mainland, contaminating the land. A horse or two killed. Some cattle lying on the shore. And a few angry crofters, wondering what the hell was going on. How that happened, we will never know. Seabirds flying from the island to the mainland. Incompetence in our procedures or the men that carried them out. But we can only come to one conclusion, Lambert, which is…?'

'Mistakes were made, sir,' John's friend responded.

'Exactly that. And we need to keep a close eye on where and when they were made. The people here may be on the edge of things. It's the main reason why we carry out tests like these in places like this. But that doesn't mean the men and women around these parts don't have eyes and ears and the necessary intelligence to work out something unusual is happening here. Will we try to bear that in mind in future? Will we, gentlemen?'

'Yes, sir.'

'We will, sir.'

'Yes, sir.'

'Good.' He gave a crisp nod of his head. 'Now, let's get back to work. The laboratory will have to be cleaned. Every corner. Every cranny. Every surface sparkling. You know how to do that, don't you?'

'Yes, sir.'

'Go to it, then.'

It was something that John hated doing, making sure there wasn't a speck of blood or fur remaining anywhere after the experiments had been completed, no trace of the spleens and lymph nodes they had removed from the dead monkeys and guinea pigs, the skin they had cut and stripped away. There were other tasks he performed in his work – noting the direction of the wind or weather, the quality of sunlight and how it affected the numbers poisoned by particular sprays or gases, how rain might or might not dilute its potency. However, he especially detested washing the Petri dishes on which the work of the scientists had taken place. It was the way the stains remained in his imagination after he had spent ages scrubbing them clean. And whenever his fingers were lathered in soap suds or soaked in distilled salt water, Lillian would be back in his head again.

She had an entirely different effect on him now compared to when he had first met her in Liverpool. Back then he was still working in Sutton Oak, near St Helens, feeling a little fouled and dirtied by his employment there, a place tainted by its long history of developing mustard and poison gases. The scars and injuries connected with that work formed a rash upon the skin of many of the workforce there, creating a shadow on their lungs, the blinding of sight, a shake and shudder in their breathing, a crippling legacy of their employment in the place. It all darkened his view, dimmed his perspective on life.

And Lillian had offered some release from all that, an uplifting and cleansing, an escape. There was something about her cheer and her ease with people that provided that, as if simply by her presence he too could be cleansed and dipped in water, made to shine and sparkle once again.

He could picture the inside of the Talbot Inn, where he had first felt that sense of release – the grubby public bar with its bare boards, old men brooding over their pints, playing dominoes on the tables before them, checking the results of the horse races, sitting with their ancient dogs for company. And the saloon bar where she worked. Its large round clock on the wall, set five minutes early in order that they might chase the customers out at nine, on the dot. The labelled bottles of ales and spirits, all glistening and shining. Polished gold of beer taps. The murmured conversations of the couples around the room. Lillian behind the counter of the bar, dipping the glasses into the soapy water filling the sink, cleansing and drying each one with the brisk rub of a dishtowel and setting it out for later. As she did this, she was half-listening to the man the locals called Billy the Lip, who was talking about the Liverpool team. He could see her blue eyes glaze over, her concentration dipping as often as she steeped pint glasses into the froth, her mind vacating her surroundings.

'They're not a great team these days, but they're not a bad one either. Should be doing a lot better than they are. Further up the league, taking on the likes of Newcastle, Blackpool and Spurs. Bert Stubbins isn't a bad player. That red head of his darts around everywhere, bobbing and weaving. Wonderful at scoring goals. But he's long past his best. You know who I think is the best one in the side these days?'

'No.'

'Billy Liddell. Hard as flint, but fair with it. Nothing frilly about the way he plays. Just simple and direct. But he never lets go. Not for an instant. Just goes on and on and on… Never stopping…'

She turned away from him, steeling herself into indifference, and walked along to the other end of the bar, just in front of the mirror advertising *Burtonwood Top Hat – Brewed and Bottled by Burtonwood Brewery.*

John leaned towards her. 'Billy Liddell's not the only one who goes on and on. Never stopping.'

'He certainly isn't,' she laughed. 'I have to listen to that every day. Yesterday, he was going on and on about Bolton Wanderers. What I don't know about Willie Moir and Nat Lofthouse.'

'Well, you've escaped this time.'

'Not for long. He'll be back. Probably talking about Everton tomorrow.'

'Not if I come here every day and try to hog your attention.'

'You're welcome to try.' She grinned. 'It would certainly be an improvement.'

She walked away again, lifting the towel at the other end of the bar, drying the glasses that had gathered there during the few moments of her escape. He heard Billy the Lip beginning to drone on once more, speaking about Liverpool's defenders, men like Bill Jones and Laurie Hughes.

'He can fairly head a ball, big Laurie. Pretty fearless at doing it, too.'

It occurred to John that he possessed at least a degree of confidence back then. For all that he sometimes resented his work as a scientific officer at Sutton Oak, using animals to check how effective sarin gas might be in warfare, he could still look into the mirror (with its image of a demented aristocrat in a top hat) and see a good-looking man at ease with himself glancing back at him. Clean, clear skin. Clean, clear teeth. Clear brown eyes. Neat brown hair. Broad shoulders. Smart clothes that showed he had a good job. It was all enough to draw Lillian's gaze towards him a few times during his time there that evening, offering a quiet smile at Billy the Lip's monologue. ('I'll tell you one thing,' John said at one point. 'He's a really good dribbler himself.') He returned her look on occasions, admiring her brightness and buoyancy, the way she spoke to people within the saloon bar, knowing instantly what kind of tone she should adopt with each customer. The tolerant mother with the likes of Billy the Lip. The dog-lover, giving scraps to grateful mutts. The flirting, joking manner in which she approached some of the younger men, including himself. The stern, commanding way she spoke to those whose drinking was becoming a little out of control. It was as if she drew a different shade from everyone she encountered within the confines of the bar. She had told him once that it all began and ended there.

'It's just a flirtation,' she had grinned, explaining it all to him. 'Most men know the rules of that particular game, how it doesn't mean very much, stays within these walls, never leaves the building. If it does, I know how to repel those who step across the boundaries. Believe it or not. I do it all the time.'

And he had been convinced by that explanation in the beginning.

It was only later he had doubts.

5

Every time anything important happened within the village, Jessie would sit down and write a letter. She did this to inform a number of people who had left the island about everything that was occurring within its borders. Sometimes it was her fellow villagers, settled, perhaps, in Toronto or Winnipeg, a town called Peterborough in central Ontario, even the pupils she had served in her years working in the school canteen. On other occasions, it was a man called Neil Mackenzie, from the nearby village of Outer Coll, who had been on the *Metagama* along with George. Neil had been the first of them to tell her that no one had seen George since the ship arrived in the New Brunswick city of Saint John.

He seemed to vanish after we landed, as if he was swallowed by the place. A few of us went to search for him everywhere but there was no sign of him. We even went to back to check if he had left the Metagama. *He had. But he disappeared soon afterwards.*

Neil had settled in a small community named Williamstown in Vermont, writing from there occasionally about his life, how he worked in the store there, having married a woman who, together with her family, had arrived in that place.

There's a fellow called John Murray, from South Dell, here. They call him Jock in these parts. He teaches in the school. Married to a woman called Avis. He always jokes about that, saying she was called after the birds.

On another occasion, he had told her:

George wasn't right when he was with us on the Metagama. *Kept talking about his brother Iain, how he was lost on the* Iolaire, *how the whole island was tinged both with his death and the loss of others. It was clear he had never got over that.*

She had wept after receiving that letter, aware that there was some truth in it, that George was obsessed with the way his brother had been taken that night. In some ways, he was not alone in this. For all they rarely spoke about it, there were many people around her who had not got over that loss. There were times when, like a handful of others in the village, she would find herself reciting in her head the Gaelic patronymics of the victims of that tragedy of 1st January 1919, the ones who came from the houses not far from her own.

'Seonaidh MhicGeoch. Mac Dhòmhaill. Iain Saighdeir. Iain Choinneach. Iain Mhoireasdain. Dòmhnall Red. Dòmhnall Eachainn. Calum Ghabsainn. Dòmhnall Ghabhsainn.'

But, despite his silence, it was mainly George to whom Jessie's letters were written. She would take out a writing pad and sit at the kitchen table beside the stove, scribbling down a quick note before she forgot about a particular incident or occasion, recording what had occurred.

Ishbal Coinneach has just passed away, she might write. *She was ill for quite some time.*

Dolina had a baby girl.

There's been a good crop of potatoes this year. The turnips are doing well, too.

In the beginning, for a year or so after George had sailed away to Canada on the *Metagama*, she hoped the day might come that she would give him the news from the village in person, face-to-face. Or even if he decided never to come back and she travelled to stay with him in Winnipeg or Toronto instead. 'What has happened to so-and-so?' he might ask. 'Any notion of how thingummyjig is getting on?' And she gave him answers to these questions, all scribbled down in the letters written in the years when they were apart. It was a way, she told herself, of protecting him in the conversations he might have with villagers. Some of them would take his ignorance as a personal insult to either themselves or their families. 'How come you didn't know my father had died? Did you forget?' Some would just find it awkward – that one of their own hadn't seen fit to keep up to date with all that was happening in the village.

The letters were also a way of preserving him in her thoughts, how kind he had been to her in school when, a few years older than her, he had helped with her arithmetic, explaining the intricacies of multiplication and division, assisting her when she struggled with her tables.

'Twelve by twelve is…?' he would say.

'Sixty-eight,' she might answer, deliberately getting the number wrong in order to hold onto his company longer.

'No. No. No,' he'd grin. 'Try again.'

There were occasions, too, when he'd turn up at her home with a bucket of fish he had caught in one of the nearby lochs or on the shoreline. Trout, perhaps, or cuddies. Her mother's smile would gleam almost as much as the catch when she took it into the house.

'He's a fine, decent lad, that one. Always kind and generous.'

And Jessie would blush when she said this, almost as much as she did when he saw him diving off the rocks near the Tràigh

Mhòr. She had watched him as he stood there, the tautness of his muscles, the dark wisps of hair in his armpit, the shadow and strangeness around his groin. All this kept surfacing in her thoughts when they spent time together, walking in the same direction home after Sunday service in the church, working in a potato field or the peats.

Later on, as the decades passed, she gave other reasons to herself. She wasn't just writing to him. She was writing a diary, her own version of the Tolsta section in the 'From the Butt to Barra' page of the *Stornoway Gazette,* a reminder to those around her – if they ever bothered to look among her belongings when she died – of all that had happened in her life.

She recalled the last date she had seen him: 21st April 1923. She had been nineteen at the time, just starting work gutting herring in Stornoway, long before her days in the school canteen. George was three years older. She recalled the way he had looked that day as they stood together below the steeple of Martin's Memorial. It was a way of avoiding the crowds that were already beginning to come together on Cromwell Street and Bayhead, gathering also near Number One Pier in Stornoway harbour, where the *Metagama* was tied up, ready to welcome the emigrants from Lewis on board alongside the Russians and Latvians who were already on the vessel. They had gone there when they first arrived in the town, hearing the prayers of some of the Jewish passengers on board echoing around the seafront.

'*Baruch atah Adonai, Eloheinu Melech ha'olam, hamotzi lechem min ha'aretz.*' ('Blessed are you, Lord our God, King of the universe, who brings forth bread from the earth.')

Someone told them that those praying had just escaped

from a massacre inflicted on their home town by Russian forces. Jessie shivered, aware that she could not cope with news like that. She sometimes shook when she saw the way certain crofters in her village behaved towards their animals, cursing and kicking their dog, failing to feed their sheep properly in winter.

'Let's go,' she whispered, taking George's arm and guiding him away from the pier towards the church where all the English speakers in the town went to sing hymns and pray. She would feel safe there – not watched closely as she so often felt while walking around Tolsta, going down to the shore to gather what the tide had washed up. There would be less chance of her father hearing that the two of them were together. 'I'd be careful about that family,' he had said once, his words measured, calm and different from her mother's. 'Not always the most reliable of souls.' She would not feel alien and strange either as she had done when she heard the strangers' prayers, all reminding her that the shores outside these islands were sometimes an uncomfortable and disconcerting place, one that might bring sudden and unexpected changes.

George's fair hair, already thinning, was hidden under a grey tweed cap. His blue eyes, bright and piercing with the tears he tried to swallow, were taking in every detail of her face. She had been pretty back then. Every time she glanced at the mirror now, nearly thirty years later, she could see a faint memory of how she had looked that day. The tangle of red hair, which one of her classmates had said made her resemble a dandelion, impossible to tie down and fasten in a bun like so many other women in the village. Pale skin. Blue eyes. The defiant tilt of her chin. Most of that had changed over the last few decades.

The sharp edge of salt-laced winds had coarsened her skin. Grey muted the shade of her hair. Even the sparkle in her gaze had dulled a little, the set of her chin softened. Yet the one thing that had never altered was the memory of the kiss he had placed on her cheek. Clumsy, short and virginal – it was a flurry and brush with the promise of sin, made more thrilling, too, by the way she was standing above him on the church steps.

'We will see each other again,' he said. 'When I can afford it, I'll send money to you. Get you the chance to come over.'

'I'll wait for that.'

'It might be a wee while. We have to work on a farm in Ontario for the first few years. Pay back our passage. After that, we can go where we want. Toronto. New York. The car factories in Detroit. I'll send you money as soon as I can, pay your passage over.'

She blushed. 'I'll do my best to be patient.'

'Good.' He gave her another clumsy kiss, this time brushing her lips. She felt its truth and tenderness, the way it made her tremble.

'And if it doesn't work out, will you be back?'

'No.' He shook his head. 'I won't be back.'

She nodded, all too aware of the rage that was within him. He had spoken about it one Friday night, when they had walked home together from church, passing the school where they had both sat behind desks, albeit a few years apart. He had talked about his older brother Iain's death on the *Iolaire*, drowned along with 200 others on the edge of Stornoway harbour on the morning of 1st January 1919; how the authorities had tried to cover up and excuse the calamity in the inquest that followed the incident; how they had failed to honour their promise of giving land to those who had fought in the war; how some men had clambered over the walls of farms like the one in nearby Gress, claiming a few acres as crofts for themselves.

'It's as if they're playing games with us all the time, as if we're designed just to be toys for the fingers of small boys.'

A moment or two later, George spoke once again, as if conscious that she was unsettled.

'But there's no need to worry about that. I'll work hard. I'll do well and bring you over there with me. I promise you that.'

'I know.'

'And it won't be too long, either. As soon as I can make it.'

She squeezed his arm, feeling the weight and quality of the jacket he was wearing. It was something that his mother had talked about, warning him that as soon as he got on the *Metagama*, he should take off his best clothes and put them in a place where neither sea nor dirt could get to them. '"You've got to look really smart when you arrive in Canada,"' he said, imitating his mother's sharp voice. '"Make a good impression on the folks there."' They had giggled when he told her this, knowing that the only reason George's mother had come out with these remarks was to try and hold her own feelings in check, choke back any possibility of tears by talking about life's practicalities.

'Do you think she wants you to stay?' Jessie asked.

'Of course. She's already lost one son. She doesn't want to lose another.'

'That's true. She's still got Angus, though.

'Aye. And she worries about him endlessly. Going out on the *Midnight Star* is not the safest way to make a living. It's as if her family is being whittled away.'

'Your dad is probably good for a few years yet.'

'Aye. I hope so. I would hate the thought of him leaving us soon after I'm gone. It would take away all her hope in life.'

George kissed Jessie once again, more this time for reassurance than longing. She felt his fingers grip her back tightly.

'I'll have to go soon,' he muttered. 'Get the medical check over with. Avoid the crush. Are you going to go down and see us leave?'

She shook her head, looking down the length of Francis Street, the large number of people gathering round the Town Hall at the foot of the hill. There were a group of men from Back, talking among themselves. She recognised Neil Mackenzie, a broad-shouldered, dark-haired man of her own age among their number. He was someone she knew – he had relations in North Tolsta – and she had sometimes been aware of him looking at her, following her every move as she worked with her father and mother nearby. It was probably for this reason that he had taken it upon himself to write to her after George had disappeared – a half-imagined closeness, an almost forgotten neighbourly bond. There was another man, too, coming up the road towards them with a length of rope he had just purchased from Charles Morrison's shop, coiled and looped around his shoulders. For a moment, the daft notion came into her head that she might snatch the rope from him and tie it round George, refusing to let him go. His absence would not be missed among the 300 or so young men and women leaving the island. There would be other boats, too, steaming out from Stornoway and the other islands for Canada. Perhaps the next time they could go together.

'I'd break down if I went and watched you leave,' she explained. 'And it's not the kind of thing you do if you come from Tolsta. You'll know that better than most.'

He laughed. 'We're not like the Stornoway folk, are we? Practiced at making exhibitions of ourselves. Not like them at all.'

He kissed her again, becoming – she thought – a little more adept each time he did so.

'I think that's why we suit one another. Same cloth we're cut from. Same kind of attitude of mind. We wouldn't get that in too many other people.'

'I know.' She grinned. 'Better bear it in mind when you've got all these fancy French girls around you in the streets of Montreal. Tell them there's someone waiting at home for you.'

'I promise I will,' he said as he kissed her one last time before making his way down to Number One Pier. 'It'll be in my head at all times.'

Blinded by tears, she didn't see much after that. Instead, she read all about what happened in the newspapers that were being passed around the village a few days later – the stories about people clambering on top of the roof of the building on Number One Pier, the pipe band playing, the Girl Guides handing out Gaelic Bibles to those going up the gangway to the ship. There was even one story that resembled her own in one of the newspapers. *Pathos of Emigrant Lovers Parting*, the headline read, with the article telling of the *Stirring Romance of Youthful Crofter Who Wants to Get Her a Home in the Great Dominion*. She cut this out diligently and carefully, along with the other stories, putting each account in an envelope with a few lines from the psalm they had sung that day in Stornoway harbour, in the hope that it might remind him of her existence:

Beum

'S e Dia as tèarmann dhuinn gu beachd
ar spionnadh e 's air treis:
An aimsir carraid agus teinn,
ar cobhair e ro-dheas.

Mar sin ged ghluaist' an talamh trom,
chan adhbhar eagail dhuinn:
Ged thilgeadh fòs na slèibhtean mòr
An buillsgean fairg' is tuinn.

God is our refuge and our strength,
in straits a present aid;
Therefore, although the earth remove,
we will not be afraid:
Though hills amidst the seas be cast;
Though waters roaring make,
And troubled be; yea, though the hills,
by swelling seas do shake.

There was a written note there, too, one that was waiting for an address, a farm somewhere in Ontario to which she could send her letter. It was the first of many she would never send, stored away in the kitchen dresser, waiting for him to let her know exactly where he was. That information never came to her. Instead, she still kept writing, telling him of all that was happening both in the village and the island as a whole. Sitting alone this evening, Jessie began to write her next letter:

Today, there is a strange vessel anchored off Tolsta Head. People have noticed all sorts of odd things about it…

6

'I hear you're up to your usual witchcraft in Tolsta,' Finlay John said to Duncan when he walked along the harbour front that day. The fisherman from Barvas was sitting on the bollard where he was usually to be found, mending nets beside his boat, the *Silver Crescent*. Over his shoulder, there were other boats to be seen. The *Minna*, the Fishery Protection Vessel. The *Larkspur*. The *Stornoway Maid*. The *Brave Venture*. A few boats from Peterhead, Fraserburgh, Kyleakin, Castlebay. Men working round and about, cleaning decks, spreading out nets, painting vessels; touching up, perhaps, the letters that differentiated one from another – SY360, PD272, FR196, CY26. A jumbled alphabet that made immediate sense to some.

'What do you mean?'

'A strange boat anchored off there. Trails of smoke. Mists and fog. Spells being cast. Some kind of cauldron on board. I even hear there's a red flag being flown.' Finlay John winked, a bright glimmer in his blue eyes as he began to hum a tune below his breath. '*Then raise the scarlet standard high / Within its shade we'll live and die / Though cowards flinch and traitors sneer / We'll keep the red flag flying here.* Who'd have thought Free Presbyterians would ever be singing that in Tolsta?'

'Very funny.'

'Well, whatever it is, it looks as if it's Top Secret. We got a note to tell us fishermen to stay out of their way, not to come too close to these waters. The Ness boat, the *Mayflower*, was warned about fishing nearby. Any notion what they're doing?'

'I have ideas.'

'And what on earth might they be?'

Duncan told Finlay John about the monkey that Jessie had carried with her from the shoreline, the little round creatures that he hadn't seen but Jessie had told him about, the strange men in their white costumes he had witnessed on the sands cleaning up the debris clustered there.

'They looked like some kind of spirits. Messengers from the dead,' he said, echoing some of the words he had heard from Jessie's lips at the time. 'The most spooky thing I've ever seen.'

Finlay John looked as if he was going to respond to this with a joke, but he stopped himself just in time, sensing, perhaps, from Duncan's mood that this wasn't a moment for laughter.

'Sounds as if it's like what happened near Aultbea. Gruinard Island,' he muttered.

'What's that?'

'Well, a woman – Margaret Ann – from our village is married to the minister there. He comes from Waternish in Skye, I think. Well, anyway, she was telling me a story she had heard from the doctor who lives next door. He's been in Aultbea for ages. Since the war, if not long before.'

Finlay John paused, and both men took in the view on the other side of the harbour. It was filled with trees, alien to this landscape and brought there a century before by Sir James Matheson, a man made rich by trading opium to the Chinese. 'A different kind of plague,' Duncan's father had said when he was alive, spitting out the words. 'But just as deadly as TB and the Spanish flu. Both of which I've seen in my lifetime.' Nevertheless, Duncan welcomed the trees' presence on the edge of Stornoway. Their rustling and shades would be in his mind when he sang Psalm 96 with the other members of the congregation in church, when, too, he wanted to escape from the island and be somewhere away from its moors and beaches.

Biodh aoibhneas air a' mhachair fòs,
is air gach nì a th'ann:
An sin bidh aiteas air gach coill'
is air gach craoibh is crann...

Let fields rejoice, and ev'ry thing
that springeth of the earth:
Then woods and ev'ry tree shall sing
with gladness and with mirth.

'These scientists working for the military took sheep from the mainland to Gruinard,' Finlay John continued, 'a bare, barren place where nobody lived. They tethered the sheep there at its western end and then they set off small explosions. Once, the military even flew a plane across, dropping a bomb there. The next thing I knew, there were all these carcasses lying on the ground. The poor beasts had breathed in the poison they'd unleashed. And then the military tried to bury them by blasting rock on top of them. No bloody good. It wasn't long before some of them were washed ashore onto the mainland. They poisoned the earth where they landed. Anthrax, apparently. A short time later, a horse, some cattle and sheep were all dead nearby. Perhaps more. Who knows what the birds that land on that island might do, where they might carry the disease? Who knows what they might *still* do?'

Finlay John shook his head, shivering as he contemplated all that had happened. Aultbea wasn't that far away from them. Some mornings they could see the silhouettes of hills and mountains that surrounded that small township. The people there spoke Gaelic just like themselves.

'Do you know what that doctor did when he discovered what had happened?'

'No,' Duncan answered.

'He took out his bagpipes. Played a tune Patrick Mor MacCrimmon wrote when a smallpox epidemic arrived in his part of Skye three hundred years ago. Someone who had been away for years brought it with him, carrying it around the church services he went to. The illness killed many people, including a lot of children. Seven or eight of MacCrimmon's own. The tune's called *Lament for the Children*. Ask someone from the pipe band to play it for you sometime. It's a really moving piece.'

He turned away from Duncan as he said this, for all that the bus driver could see his friend's eyes were sparkling.

Not with laughter this time.

But with tears.

A moment or two later, however, he was grinning again, wiping away his tears with the sleeve of his jersey. 'Not that I suppose his choice of tune made any kind of impression on the folk who were on the island at that time. They wouldn't have understood what he was trying to tell them. Just thought he was making a hell of a racket. Just thought the local doctor was making an awful lot of noise.'

7

'Shepherd's not as bad as some of the other fellows,' Lambert said. 'Granted, he can be a pompous, punctilious idiot sometimes, but he's not the worst. You should have seen the ones who were with us on Operation Harness. Bunch of bloody incompetent fools.'

John and Lambert were looking at the mainland hills as they talked, staring into the greyness of the day and wondering if they could give names to what they saw. It was all far too blurred – even the outline of Suilven unclear and indistinct. No chance, either, of seeing some of the small fishing ports they knew existed at the edge of sea lochs, tucked below the ridges of hills. These sights were lost to them in mist and cloud, depriving them of their bearings in this world. Somewhere far down south from them was the coastline of Cumbria, Lancashire, even North Wales, the places that had provided their first moorings, their first hold on life.

'There was this Scottish guy called Fielding in charge of us there. It was his bright idea to have the tests somewhere like the Bahamas, where the waters were calm and the weather was at least predictable. Not only did that not turn out to be the case, but it also turned out to be hot. Seriously hot and choppy. Can you imagine what it would be like trotting around in costumes like ours with a warm, stifling breeze gusting around you all the time? I'll tell you what, John' – he laughed – 'it's a chill wind that sometimes blows you good.'

'You can have too much of that, Mike.'

'So I've noticed. You wouldn't think it was nearly June here. Still bloody chilly. Still, it's a lot better than what we had there.'

He paused, taking a draw from his cigarette.

'They took the sheep in from Texas. Some six hundred of the blighters. Most of them were dead by the time we got to use them. The guinea pigs were nothing short of disastrous. Dead when we took them out of the cages. As for the monkeys, loads of them got pneumonia in the warm, damp atmosphere. Dead. Dead. Dead. We spent much of our time counting corpses, guarding them from the seabirds whirling around. And that was before we tested out anthrax, tularemia, brucellosis on them. What a waste of bloody time.'

Lambert chuckled, trembling as the coldness of the Minch breathed over them. There was a small boat in the distance, one that tumbled among waves, its progress slow and faltering.

'And then, of course, there were the dinghies, the *Narvik* trailing a whole lot of them across the water, all filled with sheep, guinea pigs and monkeys. God. It was bloody agony to step around them, hard to keep upright when you're making your way through the dead bodies and there's movement underneath your feet, rocking you from side to side. Damn. There were times when, with all the clowns around you, you'd think you'd wandered onto the set of a comedy show. *Mr Potts Goes To Moscow.* Laurel and Hardy. *Abbott and Costello Meet Frankenstein.*

'Sounds awful,' John mumbled. 'Glad I wasn't there.'

'But, you know, that wasn't the worst thing about the whole experience. No. That was listening to Fielding's daily sermons.

The pompous ass would stand in front of us all morning and spend ages trying to justify what we were doing. One day he'd say something like, "Don't you know that Stalin and his cronies are doing the same thing as us, that there's a laboratory somewhere on an island in the middle of the Aral Sea where his crowd of boffins are concocting their own versions of the plague, anthrax, cholera? That they carried out typhus tests in Leningrad Military Academy? We have to protect our people from that." The next day he'd be declaring, "Don't you know this is how we're going to defeat the Commies? Use these weapons and we'll leave all the buildings standing from Murmansk all the way to Vladivostok. Just walk into their factories and take over their jobs."' Lambert stopped for a moment, gathering more breath for his outrage. 'Sometimes he even used to round it all off every evening with a verse from the Bible. Isaiah 26:20. *Come, my people, enter thou into thy chambers, and shut thy doors about thee: hide thyself as it were for a little moment, until the indignation be overpast.* Pious Scottish bastard. I felt sick every time I listened to him.'

Again, he paused, trembling as he took another puff from the Capstan cupped in his hand.

'And I couldn't shake it off. I felt tarnished and fouled by it all. Do you know I couldn't touch my wife for weeks after I came back? And it wasn't because my fingers were contaminated. It was as if my heart, mind and soul were, instead. Bloody pious Scottish bastard. Bloody stupid fool.'

John shook his head, grinning weakly, willing Lambert's diatribe to come to an end. He was prone to them from time to time, and here on the *Ben Lomond* there was no escape from his words. John pushed all thought of Lambert away. And then it was worse: Lillian was back in his head again. He could no longer see Lambert and his earnest little face, all twisted as he tussled with his conscience. Instead, he could see her once more, out drinking in the Hermitage or Lime View with that dark-haired stranger whose features he couldn't quite make out. There were moments when he felt it was one of his friends – smooth and suave Matthew Dawson, perhaps, or his old neighbour, David Jenkins. Or maybe it was someone he had glimpsed in the saloon bar of the Talbot Inn, some man with whom she had flirted in much the same way as she had done with him – 'It's really great to see you. What have you been up to since you last came round?' – and he would gabble out his answers, taking in at a glance the smartness of her attire, the sweet roundness of her body. He shook the image from his mind, trying to respond to Lambert instead.

'There's a lot of these pious Scottish bastards. Tolbin took a walk round Stornoway the other day and he said the place was full of churches. One for almost every inhabitant, and some of them rather large, too. It seems there's been some kind of religious revival going on here the last year or two, chasing almost the entire population through its doors.'

'They'll need them for their prayers if they ever find out what's going on here,' Lambert muttered.

'Oh, it's going on in other places, too. All over the world.'

'Aye. But these kind of people always think they're special, that it's unique to them. Part of their nature. Ordained by their history.'

But John had lost it, unable to concentrate on his friend's words. Instead, he was thinking about Lillian again, how he didn't really trust her very much. He knew he had got some of that from his mother. Not just the old woman's words but her attitudes. She had been that way since his father had left the house, going to live with a postmistress in Wigan instead. It was a bit of a family tradition, that kind of behaviour – infecting the generations in the same way as pneumonic plague might fill the air. Her own father had deserted the household, too, disappearing to some other town or city, leaving behind his children and his job in the docks. He wondered if he had inherited that from her – either the bad judgement she had shown when she chose a partner or else the insecurity and jealousy that gnawed within him, making it impossible to trust any woman who might decide to share his life. He knew, anyway, that his mother had spotted a restlessness in Lillian, mentioning it time and time again in their conversations, much to his irritation.

'You know she's a bit of a free spirit, John. Much like your own dad. You'll rue the day yet when you got tangled up with her.'

He stiffened, clenching his fists.

'You're going to have to work hard to keep a hold of her.' She paused before coming to another judgement. 'And then there's her religious background. That'll come to the fore sometime. These people always revert to type.'

'What do you mean?' He blinked.

'Her parents are regular churchgoers, she told me. Heavy evangelical types. You can run all you like from something like that, but you can never quite hide.'

He shook his head. He hadn't quite registered the impor- tance of that, though she had mentioned it in conversation. '*Mum and Dad are strong believers. They take every word in the Bible dead seriously. I used to hate that when I was young.'*

'We'll be fine,' he muttered. 'Just you wait and see.'

'Oh, I will. Don't you worry. I will.'

However much he tried to chase the thought from his mind, he could see the truth of his mother's words. He had been aware of them every time he saw Lillian at work in the saloon bar, how she gave so much time to the men whose gazes were so like his own, following her movements as she filled pints of beer, washed an array of glasses. There was a tolerance in her, an indulgence towards others and their flaws. Sometimes he interpreted this darkly, seeing dishonesty and deceit in her glance. At other moments, she shone. He saw her kindness coming through, as if her own character was being cleansed every time she dipped these glasses into soapy water, making sure they sparkled and shone. She even listened to the likes of Billy the Lip as he moved onto talk about the best players for Newcastle United, Burnley or Sunderland FC, aware, perhaps, that at the end of his monologue there would be a reward. Or maybe it was her innate affection for others. He could never quite decide.

'Go and buy one for yourself,' Billy the Lip would grin after he had spent time with her.

And this all followed a pattern. Her eyes flashed and brightened every time a man squeezed a tip in her fingers. A half-crown. A florin. A ten-shilling note. The kind of cash every bar-girl depended on to make a proper living from the job. Even Eric, the pub landlord, adopted the same behaviour. John felt he moved too close to her as they shifted through the narrow space between the bar and counter, as if he were unaware his own wife Lucy's eyes were on them, judging the proximity in which they operated, making sure they did not have too much freedom to misbehave. He was a man, after all, who had a bit of a reputation with the ladies. According to Lillian, he had difficulty keeping his eyes and hands away from them. Especially when he had taken a drink.

'She's really good,' Eric said to John one time. 'The pub really fills up when she's on duty. Earns every penny of her bonus.'

John could see that – the couples sitting round the tables whispering and talking to one another, the shuffle of a crowded floor, some dockers and a group of Irishmen in the bar next door singing about the delights of going back to Donegal, a pair of businessmen drinking too much after their day in the office. All of them appeared to be involving her in their discussions as she stepped out from behind the counter and wiped the tables, clearing ashtrays and lifting empty glasses.

'It's good to see you, Lillian.'

'Here. Take this for yourself.'

It was as if the entire world knew this was the best way to win over the girl he wished to woo and marry. She smiled too easily at others, and he would sit at the counter brooding over his pint of beer, watching her every move as he talked to some of the acquaintances he had made there. There was Jack, who loved to do the cryptic crossword in the *Guardian*, leaning towards him from time to time when he was puzzled about a clue.

'Rewrite article for narration… Seven letters. What would that be?'

Billy, who came from Glasgow and loved to talk about Rangers and Celtic all the time – how much better it was going to see them than Anfield Road or Goodison.

And then there was a retired fisherman called Geoff Phillips who – just like Lillian – came from Fleetwood. He would speak about the lighthouses in the town, how there was nowhere quite like it. He enjoyed talking, too, about the fishing boats that were tied up at Wyre Dock, reciting their names as if they were part of a prayer.

'The *Kingfisher. Silver Harvest. Melody. Carella. Sweet Home. Majestic…*' He would interrupt himself then. 'Lillian has a relative on the *Carella*. Don't you, girl?'

Lillian would grin back at him. 'I do. A first cousin.'

'See. I told you, John. There's salt in her veins.'

'Oh, he knows that, Geoff,' Lillian would laugh. 'He's more worried about the salt on my tongue.'

John recalled the moment a year or so later when he met that relative in Lillian's family home in Fleetwood. The man – Dave Callaghan – was just back from a fishing trip to Iceland, his grip wrapping as tightly round his hand as any fishing net.

'So you're the one who my cousin's got her hooks into,' he'd said, laughing.

And then Dave had spoken to Lillian, his words reminding John of that aspect of her life she rarely spoke about, the fact that she came from a family of Evangelical Christians, where being teetotal was the norm.

'You still dabbling in the wrong kind of spirit, Lillian? Isn't it time you put that aside?'

She flushed in response. 'There may come a time. But not yet.'

'I hope so, my girl. I truly hope so. But you can't put off the hour forever.'

John had felt more comfortable when they were out of

the Talbot, away from its squash and cram of customers. She was too much at ease there, too much in control of the situation. Even when the voices of her customers grew loud and hectoring, their pitch and volume increased by the quantities of alcohol they swirled down, she seemed able to take command of everything that occurred within the walls of the bar. It was different when they went to other bars – the Hermitage, perhaps, or the Lime View – or strolled down the street together. That kindness of hers seemed safer there. She would talk to children, stop to pet dogs, take note of the presence of a cat perched on a wall, a budgie or parrot in the window of a house. She'd cling to his arm and they would talk about the work he was going to be doing in Porton Down, when he moved there in the next few months after leaving Sutton Oak. She might question him about it; he would remain tight-lipped, telling her it was mainly to do with animals, the effect of certain substances on their bodies, anything else that came to mind.

'Examining how enzymes work in their digestive systems. The effect of various substances on their spleens and lymph nodes. Things like that. Almost like a vet. There are times, too, when we do important work preparing for the possibility of pandemics. If there was one threatening the country, we'd be the first line of defence, creating vaccines, working hard to find cures for any dangerous illnesses that might come our way. You never know the day or the hour.'

He knew her eyes would dim and dull when he spoke about matters like these. Most people's did. Instead, he tried to divert her by watching her gaze following the cars that were either going past or parked by the roadside. The Ford Consul.

Hillman Minx Mark V Saloon. Austin A30. Her eyes gleamed almost as much as the sheen and polish of these vehicles, noting every detail, the tilt of wing-mirrors, her own face reflected from windscreens.

'In a year or two, I'll be able to afford one of those,' he smiled. 'The work's steady and dependable. The pay is good.'

'What's Salisbury like, then? If I went there, would there be work for me?'

'Plenty,' he assured her. 'Lots of good drinking establishments. A good few restaurants. Visitors come to see the cathedral, Stonehenge.'

'Oh, that's good,' she'd smile.

He loved her most when they sat in the cinema. She possessed a talent for quietness in its darkness. Settling in her seat, she would become engrossed in whatever film happened to be shown, occasionally pinching his arm when she became alarmed or tense. They went to a number together – *The Third Man, Captain Horatio Hornblower, The Lavender Hill Mob* – but most of those he really remembered her enjoying were those which had a female character at their centre. Barbara Stanwyck in *No Man of Her Own.* Joan Crawford in *The Damned Don't Cry.* And especially Anne Baxter and Bette Davis in *All About Eve.*

'Fasten your seatbelt,' she kept saying when she started her shift at the Talbot the following day. 'It's going to be a bumpy night.'

He should have taken that as a slogan for their entire life together.

8

'Is that it?' Mairead looked at the creature lying in the old shoe-box Jessie had placed it in.

It was curled there with its mouth open, sharp white teeth protruding from its lower jaw. Its fur had become matted and fringed with salt since being washed up on the beach, its eyes wide open as if it were alarmed. Mairead recoiled from the sight. Shuddering, she pushed the box away, flapping her hand towards her neighbour to make sure she slammed the lid tight shut.

'It looks like a baby!'

'I know. Duncan said that was the reason they used them for tests. Resembled the body of a human being more than any other animal.'

'I don't want to know these things.' Mairead shivered. 'The only thing that matters is whether it came off the boat.'

'What?'

'Are you sure that's where it came from?'

Jessie stared at her old friend, someone whom she had worked alongside in the school canteen for years. It was hard to believe that Mairead was someone who had once been in the same situation as her. In April 1923, she too had accompanied her man – Donald Gillies, from the village of Skigersta at the northern end of Ness – to Stornoway to see him off on the *Metagama*. The two women had wept together often since then, either when they travelled on the bus to town or walked down the road to the northern end of Tolsta, talking of the day they would sail across the Atlantic to meet with their partners. But their respective experiences had turned out differently. In Jessie's case, as Neil had told her, there had been silence from the moment George had stepped on the quay in Saint John, New Brunswick. Only rumours trailed after him. 'He's been seen in Detroit,' someone would whisper. 'He's in San Francisco,' another might say. And then, most cruel of all: 'He drowned himself in Lake Huron. He never managed to get over his brother's death on the *Iolaire*. Couldn't cope over there.' Jessie steeled herself each time she heard a tale like that, walking across the moor for hours. It got worse after her mother and father died – the words echoing in the silence of her cottage. She would go as far as Muirneag, Loch na Cloich, Loch Sanndabhat to escape them, lifting up plants and flowers – such as dwarf willow, rose root and English stone-crop by the shore – as she went upon her way.

Mairead's tale was different. In the beginning, for the first four years or so, she had received letters from Donald that told, first of all, how he was working on a farm in Ontario, a place where the landscape was both terrifying and unfamiliar, where he imagined he could hear wolves howling at night, bears trampling the undergrowth; where, when the snow fell, it would cover everything, blasting the windward side of trees, even the occasional boulder that jutted out from the land. Ice, too, cloaked water, all except the occasional trickle in a crack in the land. Later, his letters revealed that he had obtained employment in a factory in Toronto.

It's not the greatest of places and I miss home a lot, he had written, *but at least it's a job.*

And then there was silence. It only came to an end when a man from the village of Adabrock, a short distance away from Tolsta, came to visit his relatives.

'Gillies is back at home,' the Nessman declared. 'And he's brought a woman with him. All the way from Ontario. It seems she's a native woman from some tribe or other over there. She's expecting at the moment. I wonder how she's going to fit in over here, just beside the sea, not a tree in sight.'

'But what on earth brought them back here?'

'Oh, the Depression. The fact that he didn't have a job. As he says himself, when you don't have a job in Lewis, you don't starve. Over there, it can be entirely different. No one's looking out for you. Even when you resent the way they poke their noses into your business in these parts, at least they're doing that!'

His cousins nodded, understanding the truth of his words. They had heard stories of a man from Bragar who had come back on the *Loch Seaforth* a short time ago, returning to these shores from Canada. By the time he arrived, he didn't have a penny in his pocket. There were no soles left on his shoes.

It's a hard life over there, they decided, one of them using a phrase they had heard from their parents years before: '*Chan e òr a h-uile rud buidhe, chan e uighean a h-uile rud bàn.*' ('All that's yellow is not gold, and all white objects are not eggs.')

Mairead had wept when she discovered that – the thought of the man she loved being with some foreign woman a few miles to the north; how, too, he had betrayed her with the vows and promises he had made in his letters.

It won't be long till we are together, he had written only a couple of months before he had sailed home. *I am putting a little money aside each week to bring you across the Atlantic, joining me here.*

When she visited Jessie's home, Mairead would rant and shout about it for ages, yelling out obscenities, explaining exactly what she would do a certain part of his anatomy if she ever saw him again. There were times when Jessie would be concerned that the people of Kinlochbervie and Scourie on the other side of the Minch might hear her, that the fishermen on their boats in Broadbay could be disturbed, their fingers faltering as they laid down their nets.

'No wonder no one's going to look out for you, Gillies! Not if you're going to behave like that! You're just a tramp of a man! A bloody tramp!'

'Shhh, Mairead… People might hear you,' Jessie would warn her. 'You've got to keep your dignity!'

'Aye. Like he did! Like he bloody did!'

Yet, over the years, she altered, becoming quieter and more reserved, a little more like Jessie had reacted when she did not hear from George. In the beginning, Jessie walled herself off from others, especially men, believing she needed to be faithful to her lost one. Later, it was her own grief and sorrow that created a boundary which the local men did not venture near or cross. For all her good looks, the way in which she was capable of working on the croft tending crops and her father's flock, she was considered unstable and troubled, someone people had to be wary of approaching. It took years for her to settle, to be considered one whom a bachelor or widower could marry, find space for within his bed. By that time, it was too late for the children a crofter would expect from his wife.

Similar changes had occurred in Mairead. It was difficult to imagine her coming out with oaths and curses these days. She was the one whom the village often turned to in an emergency. When a man had been wounded – cut, perhaps, by the blade of a scythe he had been wielding. Or a child had fallen from the face of a rock. She was also good with animals, helping cattle give birth, treating sheep. There were other changes, too. She was one of those who had been caught up in the Revival, gaining sustenance and strength from her faith and the people around her in church.

Whenever the name of Donald Gillies was mentioned these days, she'd react in the same way: 'It was God's will that we are not together,' she'd declare.

Or: 'Donald has his own ways these days. I have mine.'

She would smile and shake her head in wonder at this, having heard rumours that whenever time and opportunity presented themselves, Donald would display a great fondness for alcohol.

'It would not have been a life for me. Not with him. Nor the Great Lakes in Canada. God blessed me by keeping me here instead.'

Despite this, she was still recognisably the same person she always was – dark-haired, large-limbed, uncomfortable and clumsy in her movements, a smattering of pale freckles on her skin – but so much else about her had changed. Where once she had been rebellious and restless, nowadays she was quiet and conservative, going to church a few times every week, nodding each time a minister or one of the elders said anything, whether they were right or wrong. With the greying of her hair, there had come the greying of her personality.

Yet the women of the church appreciated her presence. They would visit her home near Beinn Thearabert often, free to talk within its walls without being accompanied by their men.

'What?' Jessie blurted out finally in response to her question about where the monkey had originated.

'The boat off Tolsta Head. Are you sure that's where the animal came from?'

'Yes.'

'You've said there were other animals lying on the sand. What kind?'

Jessie shrugged. 'I've no idea. They looked like small, tubby rats.'

'No one else saw them?'

'No. Just me.'

'Not even Duncan?'

'No. These odd-looking men in their white suits were cleaning them up by then.'

Mairead clicked her tongue in satisfaction. 'So no one saw these wee round rats but you?'

'No.'

There was the longest silence there had ever been between them. No noise except the ticking of her parents' clock above the stove, a smattering of rain upon the window.

'One of the elders believes the monkey may have washed all the way here from the coast of Africa,' Mairead said.

'No.'

'And why not? These things have happened before. Last year, a bottle with a message in it was washed up on Garry. All the way from Newfoundland.'

'It's not the same thing.'

'No? And there was a tree landed on the Tràigh Mhòr the other winter. Goodness knows where that came from.'

Jessie shook her head, unable to speak. She knew what she felt like doing – to let loose screams of condemnation, cries of contradiction, perhaps hurl something in Mairead's direction, the clock above the stove, the picture with the words *Christ is the Head of this house; the Unseen Guest at every meal; the Silent Listener to every conversation* that her mother hung on the wall years before. But she knew it wasn't really within her, to lose control like that. Instead, there was a longing to set off to the moor, maybe to stay in the shielings at Dìobadal a little to the north (for all that she had heard some of the men from the *Ben Lomond* sometimes went there). Anything to avoid the complexities and difficulties of dealing with folk.

'So, are you sure? That the monkey wasn't washed here from Johannesburg, Nairobi, some place like that? The power of the sea is an amazing force.'

Jessie stiffened, recognising the names of these places as locations where Mairead's own brother had served in the Merchant Navy during the war, bringing supplies from those distant African ports to this country – the familiarity of the words a sign, perhaps, that the family had been talking about her.

'Are you sure?' Mairead repeated.

'Yes. I'm sure.'

'Definitely?'

'Yes.' She shook her head. 'You think I'm making this all up?'

'Perhaps. It's possible.'

'What do you mean?'

'Well, you have behaved strangely before. People notice these things.'

She felt herself shake and tremble. 'That was nearly thirty years ago. In most places it would have been long forgotten. But not here. Not in Lewis.'

'Probably not in other places, either. When someone behaves like that anywhere, it tends to stay in people's minds.'

'Really?'

'Really.'

Staring at her friend, Jessie stood up from her chair. 'I want you to leave,' she said. 'I want you to get out of that door and never come back.'

Mairead coloured, her hand waving as frantically as it had done when she wanted to squeeze the shoe-box tightly shut, to hide away what was contained there. 'Are you sure? After all the years we've been friends.'

'Yes. I'm sure,' Jessie declared. 'Just as I'm sure about what was washed up on the Tràigh Mhòr. Just as I know what was there.'

'After all the years we've been friends?'

'Yes. After all these years.'

Mairead's whole body shook, her clumsiness returning. Snuffling back tears, she bumped against her chair as she rose. 'I'm sorry,' she said. 'I'm sorry.'

She was out of the house before the words stumbled out of her lips, chased there by the fierceness of Jessie's gaze. The entire house trembled as she slammed the door. It took Jessie a while to recover after that. She gripped the table. She swayed back and forth. And all the time she kept thinking that she might have done the wrong thing. The two of them were old friends. They shared secrets together. They even experienced a similar loss, a gaping absence in their lives. She recalled evenings where they had spent hours in each other's company, talking about the songs of Archie Grant, which the headmaster often played on the record player bought for the pupils – *Seòlaidh Mise Null* and *Gad Chuimhneachadh* echoing around the houses of the village. Together, they had sat and learned songs that they had overheard being taught to the pupils in the school – ones like *Fàili, fàili, fàili ho ro,* written by Murdo Macfarlane, from the village of Melbost, who had spent some years in Manitoba in Canada between the wars. And *Eilean Beag Donn a' Chuain*, which looked back at the losses of the Great War. It had been created by a man who had been on the *Metagama*. They had looked together at the words they'd scrawled down on a sheet of paper from a school blackboard, trying to master the tune.

Hì rì o rì rì, togaidh sinn fonn
Air Eilean beag donn a' chuain;
Eilean beag Leòdhais, dachaigh nan seòid
A chumas an còmhrag suas;
Eilean nan tonn a dh'àraich na suinn
'S a chuidich an Fhràing gu buaidh,
Còmhla ri chèile togaidh sinn fonn
Air Eilean beag donn a' Chuain.

Hì rì o rì rì, we will raise a tune
To the little brown isle of the sea;
The isle of Lewis, home of the brave
Leading freedom to victory;

Isle of the waves that raised the heroes
And restored France to liberty
O together let us raise a tune
To the little brown isle of the sea.

Jessie's eyes filled as she recalled all this, the long friendship the two of them had lost.

9

Duncan was driving past Gress cemetery with its old crumbling chapel when Eachainn slipped down to the front of the bus. He saw the white-haired, black-suited figure in his rearview mirror, making his way from a seat near the back, his presence casting a shadow on the glass. For all that the old man was a decent, kind individual, he was also an exceptionally gloomy one, straining to see any good in the world through his thick, round spectacles. Originally from the west side of Lewis, he now lived at the edge of Duncan's village, in New Tolsta, in the handful of houses built there in the 1920s. For that reason, Duncan groaned inwardly. He knew he would be forced to share his company till the very end of his route.

'You all right?' Duncan asked, shifting gears.

'Aye. I was just at the funeral yesterday of a cousin over in Breasclete. Poor man. He never got over the battle of the Dogger Bank. He was on the *Lion* at the time. Standing on the deck when bits of steel lashed all around him. All caused by German guns. One of the pieces gashed his head. He was never the same again.' He shook his head. 'To be honest, it's a bit of a release for his wife now he's gone. He was getting worse with the years.'

Duncan shuddered. He recalled something like this from his days in Gibraltar: some of the men from the Black Watch lifting and relaying around three hundred anti-tank mines near the border with Spain. One exploded, setting the others off. Three men were killed; others injured. Included among them was his friend, Jamie. His head had been scarred and wounded when the old Admiralty Wireless Telegraph Station had been damaged in the blast. He had never been right since that day. When they took him back to his home town, Forfar, he didn't even recognise the place, wandering its streets as if he was marooned in a foreign port. Duncan shook his head at the memory.

'That must have been hard for you,' he muttered to the old man.

'It was. It was. He was my best friend at school. The two of us lived near the lightkeepers' station in the village. The one where the Flannan Isles men lived when they were off duty. We used to play together all the time with their children.'

Duncan said nothing. Instead he wondered why so many men would mention the war when there were no women present. They never did when they were there. He shook his head again, taking the bus around a clutch of sheep that stayed fixed on the road, refusing even to recognise the presence of the vehicle. Fortunately, unlike his time in Gibraltar, he could squeeze the horn to make sure they scattered, being sent upon their way.

'I suppose that's why so many men from Breasclete became lightkeepers,' he said. 'It was all so familiar to them.'

'Aye. Part of our lives. It took the men from the village places, too. Fair Isle. Pentland Skerries. Bell Rock. Ailsa Craig. Holy Isle. Every corner of Scotland.'

Duncan slowed the bus once more, winding through another gathering of sheep. For some reason they all seemed to be drawn to the roadside today. 'And none of them ever disappeared?'

'Och, no,' Eachainn growled in his usual manner. 'That Flannan Isles story has gone a bit wild since that silly Englishman wrote the poem. While it's true that three men went missing, there's little in his verse except gossip and rumour. Stuff and nonsense.'

'It's what makes the world go round, they say...' Duncan laughed, his attention still upon the road.

Eachainn frowned, fiddling with his black tie as if it were fastened too tight for his scrawny, wrinkled neck. Like most men in the village, he wasn't used to wearing one. Most of the time he was clothed in a woollen jumper and a pair of dungarees. Duncan had seen him many times, a thin, compact figure, digging potatoes, cutting peat not far from the roadside. He would give him a toot as his bus went past, gaining in return a wave of a dirt-blackened hand.

'You know I worked as a ghillie in Gairloch after the Great War?'

'No.'

'Something happened there when I was in these parts. Eight men died one day after they went fishing on Loch Maree. Most were guests in one of the local hotels. Some of them were ghillies like myself. There were terrible rumours going round at the time. That the military were testing out gas around Loch Maree and Beinn Eighe. That the Yanks had left some poison pellets in the area after they had left their base in Kyle during the war. That one of the people present in the group was a spy and that some Russians – or even Germans – had tried to poison him. A lot of weird stories were told.'

'And?'

'It all turned out to be food poisoning. Botulism, I think they called it. Caught from eating a duck. Paste of some sort. The rest of it was all rumour, gossip, stuff and nonsense.'

Duncan kept quiet. He knew what the old man was trying to tell him – that chatter like this was rife in small communities. Hell! Did he need to be told that? He knew it not only from his life in Tolsta but also from his days locked away in Gibraltar. One minute, they were about to be blasted by artillery guns from Spain, all lined up across the border in La Línea, eager to reclaim these heights of limestone rock as part of their own territory, making their nation complete. The next, Italian planes would be soaring towards them from the east, hoping to put an end to the way British troops guarded the exit and entrance to the Mediterranean, making their mastery over that ocean complete. Or it might be a German U-boat sneaking into their harbour, out to sink vessels from the Royal Navy. Or a squadron from Vichy France, smarting at the hurt the Royal Navy had caused them when they sank their ships in French Algiers in 1940, killing nearly a thousand of their sailors. Or so-and-so was a spy, an enemy agent. A servant, a trade unionist. One of these Socialists whose forces had been defeated in the Civil War across the border. A supporter of Franco or the Spanish monarchy, plotting revenge, a way of reclaiming Gibraltar as part of their territory, the land they had lost. Wasn't that one of the reasons why they had shipped out thousands of ordinary people from their homes in the Rock, to prevent stories like that whirling around like the Levant cloud that sometimes fell there, misting its narrow, winding streets?

It wasn't until the bus reached the post office at the north end of North Tolsta that Eachainn spoke again, his words slow and precise.

'We have to be very sure, Duncan, before we speak about things like the dead monkey you and Jessie are said to have seen on the sands, the trail of gas that's supposed to be rising from the boat. People are frightened by the story. Old people are staying indoors. A few parents are not allowing their children to play on the Tràigh Mhòr or Garry. All terrified by tales of poison or finding monkeys and rats upon the beach. You can understand that, Duncan. Can't you? And the truth of it is that the men on this ship might be doing these tests for good reasons. Most people around here know another war is probably on its way, that we have to be prepared for whatever the Russians or some other idiot might throw at us. You can understand that, too, Duncan. Can't you? You can understand that?'

Again, he didn't speak. He was angry at the injustice of all this. For all that he often heard stories, whether in the library or at the Club Bar or Mac's Imperial, he wasn't a man who let secrets slip from his mouth too easily. He had heard all sorts of rumours over the years – that the government was planning to build an atomic station somewhere in the Highlands, that they had the notion of creating a missile range somewhere in the Outer Hebrides, even the idea of using Kyle of Lochalsh as a submarine base. Never, though, had he passed on these tales. His training, his years working in Gibraltar, had taught him not to behave like that.

'I'm sorry, Duncan,' Eachainn said when the bus stopped at his home. 'I just had to say these things.'

'Listen,' Duncan hissed as he squeezed on the handbrake. 'I saw the dead monkey Jessie had in her arms. I saw the men in white suits cleaning up the mess that was lying there. If it wasn't rats and monkeys they were tidying away, what was it?' He shook his head in disgust. 'You tell me. What the hell was it?'

10

Tolbin was on the deck as John made his way out that morning. Binoculars fixed to his gaze, he was scanning the horizon for birds, scribbling down the names of those present in a notebook stuffed in his pocket. The other one had a field guide squashed within it, in case he couldn't identify any he had seen. The only thing that altered was the direction in which he looked. He'd swirl around from time to time. Mainly it was towards Tolsta, Cellar Head or the length of the beach, the Tràigh Mhòr. He had spotted a group of sandwich terns there the other day, recognising the bird's piercing cry, its tufted black cap, grey wings, the piercing pliers of its yellow bill, how it plunged into the waves, almost imitating the shape of its beak as it did so. He nudged John as he watched it, handing him his binoculars.

'Here! Take a look at it,' he said.

John did as he was asked, seeing the silver of an eel in the beak of one of the birds. It looked like the bird was drooling, its meal brimming over as it tried to gulp down more than it could eat. He handed the binoculars back.

'This is a marvellous place to be, for someone like me,' Tolbin declared. 'I'd pay good money to be here.' He chuckled wryly to himself, his dark face gleaming, his broad chest heaving with excitement. 'And they're paying me!'

John knew little about Tolbin's background; just the fact that when he travelled to Stornoway to help with a further load of monkeys and guinea pigs, he was the one who noted that the place was full of churches, more than he'd ever seen in any small town before. 'It's like Heinz's 57 Varieties,' he'd declared. 'One – at least – for every week of the year.' After that, Lambert had whispered to John, 'His time there would have made him uncomfortable. Tolbin's Jewish, don't you know? More used to synagogues than churches.'

Today, he was looking towards the mainland, the slopes of Stac Pollaidh and the twin peaks of Suilven, the outlines of Quinag, Cul Mor and Cul Beag clear in the morning light, growing more distinct each dawn as midsummer crept upon them, apart from the occasional morning they were blurred by rain or mist. Even during these hours, Tolbin stayed focused, his delight in being in all this emptiness unaffected by the smirr of rain, lifted by the possibilities and proximity of birds either snuggled down in cliffs or soaring, the chance of seeing dolphins, seals or whales. Today, however, the sea was blue, its surface unscratched by waves.

'There's a place out there called Handa Island. It's mentioned in the guide books. No one lives there – everybody left years ago. Loads of guillemots and razorbills nest there on its sandstone cliffs and stacks. A few puffins, too. It's a place I'd love to go to. Do you think we could ask Shepherd to go out there, sail a little closer to its cliffs?'

'You could try.'

'And get nowhere. I know just what his answer would be.'

'We could pass it on our way home in October.'

'Hah! I know what the crew would say if I suggested the likes of that. There would be mutiny on the *Bounty*.'

'Yes. And you'd be Captain Bligh.'

'Thank you, Mr Christian. You may proceed.' Tolbin raised his binoculars again, staring at the horizon.

Out there, near one of the local fishing boats, the name *Silver Crescent* painted on its side, John could see a group of white birds veering upwards before plunging deep into the sea. For some reason he thought of Lillian, their wedding day in Emmanuel United Church in Fleetwood, the white veil being lifted from her face by a gust from the sea, as if a mist was concealing her features for an instant. There would have been a few fishermen at the service that day, her mother's people, all familiar with this landscape, able to put names to these birds, find fish within these waters. One of them had told John he had been fishing off the shores of Iceland, catching shoals of cod within their nets. He hadn't a clue where to take that conversation, as if he too was circling like some of the seabirds he watched overhead, unable to touch land.

'Here! Take that! Have a squint.' Tolbin shoved the binoculars in John's direction, pointing a finger in the direction of the sea, too.

When he lifted the binoculars, he saw a puffin flying just above the water. He could see its harlequin beak, its tiny head with its sad eyes, the way it looked as if it were wearing a tuxedo, wings beating in a frenzy. It looked – in some ways – human, as if it were going against its nature by becoming airborne, intent on staying aloft.

'Amazing,' John said. 'Something to tell my grandchildren about.'

'They're comical-looking birds. They don't look as if they should be able to fly.'

'No. They don't.' He handed back the glasses to Tolbin

again. 'You know what I don't get about you?'

'What?'

'You're a man who obviously loves nature. More than anything else. Yet you're here. Experimenting with animals. Monkeys. Guinea pigs. Sometimes sheep.'

Tolbin glanced in his direction. 'You think there's a contradiction?'

'Some people would say so.'

'Well, they might be right. But see it from my point of view…'

'Which is?'

'However much I love these seabirds, I hate and distrust Russians more.'

They stood for a moment, allowing these words to resound. All they were aware of was the screech of some seabird nearby, the voices of men a dull monotone behind them, the stillness of the sea like the swish of a cloth.

'Why?'

'Oh. That's easy. My ancestors fled Russia in 1906 after soldiers killed many of the Jews living there. That's why we came to this country. For all that there's been one or two bumpy moments, crazy men like Mosley and his kind, we've been more or less safe here. That's not true of my fellow Jews in Russia. Or Poland. Or Germany. Much worse for them there. Besides, we're not getting the full truth of what's happening within Russia's borders. We're not told the half. They're experimenting with chemical and biological weapons all over the place. And what else would we expect with murdering bastards like Stalin and Beria in charge? In the Solovetsky Islands, they're working with typhus, Q-fever, glanders. Somewhere else their Ministry of Agriculture is concocting another range of delights. And why not? They've got thousands of prisoners in their camps they can test these things out on. And no one's going to be any the wiser. Nobody's going to complain.'

He paused, drawing breath, preparing, too, to raise his binoculars again.

'So if you ask me whether we are right to be testing pneumonic and bubonic plague on these animals here, there's only one possible answer. Yes. Yes. Yes. We may not like doing it but we've little bloody choice. Not if we want to protect ourselves. Just like the Yanks are doing in places like Edgewood and Redstone. Preparing for the next war if or when it comes. Protecting ourselves against the next nutcase that might come along. Like Mussolini spraying Ethiopia with tons of mustard gas. Or Hitler or Stalin. And what's a monkey or a guinea pig's life compared to the like of that.'

John's head kept reeling after this. More than the swirling of birds. More than the sweep of shoals as they swam up and down the Minch, a silver flash, a shadow they could see in the water just beside the *Ben Lomond*. He couldn't help thinking about the clash of opinions among those he worked with on the boat: how the likes of Lambert found the entire notion of experimenting on animals repugnant, whereas others – Shepherd and Tolbin, for instance – thought that what they were doing was necessary to ensure their freedom, to keep them safe from the attention of Stalin and his friends. All their words stirred around his head as if it were one of the cauldrons found hanging around the vessel at various points, unsettled by waves, reminding him of the name of their exercise, their purpose in these waters. He found it hard to decide whether their presence here was for evil or good, the argument within him in the darkness of the quarters he shared with others, tripping towards him, too, in the light of day.

For once, he welcomed the way Lillian came into his thoughts. He felt himself remembering their early days in Salisbury, how they had set up a new home near to where he worked in Porton Down, how their first few months had been full of laughter and dancing, the lilt and lift of love. It was the songs he could remember from that time together. Those nights in the Old Oak Inn in the city, the Majestic Dance Hall. They could hear all sorts of music there: Patti Page's *Tennessee Waltz*, Bill Snyder's *Bewitched, Bothered and Bewildered*, Teresa Brewer's *Music! Music! Music!* And *The Thing*, by Phil Harris. Lambert had recalled that particular song when they arrived back on board the *Ben Lomond* after going to the beach. Since then, snippets from its opening verse had come again and again to John's mind, echoing through his thoughts. Something about finding a big wooden box in the bay, opening it up and discovering 'a (boom-boom-boom) right before my eyes'.

And then there was that American song by the Ames Brothers, which contained the question he had asked himself a thousand times during his and Lillian's time together in Salisbury. He'd catch her looking in the direction of some other man when they were together in the Old Oak Inn, paying attention to his every movement, the swirl of his hand, how he held himself as he stood before the bar.

'Penny for your thoughts?' he'd ask.

She would laugh then, placing a kiss on his lips, his cheek, once even his forehead.

'Only how lucky I am to be with you.'

And he would allow that gesture to deceive him, to pacify and reassure him despite the turmoil caused by the doubts thundering through his head. At the same time, though, he'd hear the melody and lyrics of that song. It created its own uncertainty in the way its singers asked whether anyone can explain the thrill of a kiss.

He knew only too well it had the power to befuddle and confuse him.

11

'Don't worry about what Mairead said,' Jessie's neighbour Seonaid declared as they worked in the peats together. 'She's just like a lot of people in the village at the moment. Very anxious and worried. There's a lot of men away working on the Hydro. Or in the Merchant Navy. They'd like them to be around and with them at all times. Especially just now.'

Jessie nodded, aware that she was telling the truth. She had heard stories of what sometimes happened when the men were working on the dams. The occasional accidents. Unexpected rockfalls. Explosions going wrong. She knew, too, that it wasn't the men from Ness or Tolsta who normally suffered the consequences of incidents like these, but the Irish or the Poles. Desperate to establish a new and better lives for themselves, they were the ones who volunteered to be 'Tunnel Tigers', to carry dynamite through cracks and chasms in the rock for the sake of a few extra pounds in their pockets. Sometimes, they suffered the consequences of their actions, their bones and guts colouring fissures, becoming embedded in stone, forever encased in the rock and cement of the new country to which they had come.

And then there were those – like Seonaid's husband, Murdo – working for the Denholm or Clan Line. Sometimes they might become lost, too. An accident in Cape Town. Washed from the deck of a tanker in the Persian Gulf. Or like the man from Tong she had heard about. He had stepped onshore from his boat in Wellington, New Zealand, never to be seen again. The tales she had heard about him resembled those she had heard about George a quarter century before:

'Someone overheard Gaelic being spoken in a bar in Auckland.'

'A woman from Ness saw him in Christchurch.'

'He was seen in Otago Harbour. He's living in Dunedin and working on a ferry boat out there.'

'He's out in Queensland, Australia, with a Greek wife.'

She shook each time she heard someone speak like that, the memories of her loss coming fresh to mind: the stories of San Francisco, Detroit, Lake Huron that had echoed from foolish mouths. It was the last tale that carried most conviction. They even mentioned the place-name, Sarnia, where George had apparently jumped from the Blue Water Bridge on the border between Canada and the United States. Someone had tried to save him but had failed to reach in time.

'Poor soul. He must have been desperate.'

'He never got over his brother's death.'

'He always was a weak and fragile man.'

Seonaid pushed down the peat-blade, heaving out the next segment from the bank. They were on the second row now, building a wall of turf at the edge of the ridge they were cutting in this part of the moor. For all that Seonaid was a thin wisp of a woman, strands of fair hair continually escaping from the tight wrap of her scarf, she was quick and nimble, as brisk and eager as she had been when she and a few others used to trek across the moor to dance on the breakwater at Port of Ness; the notes of a battered accordion echoing through the twilight there, steps dancing over cement, the whoops and hollers of those taking part. Nowadays, it was mainly the cries of a few seagulls that accompanied them, her feet confined in wellington boots, soiled by earth and peat, the smell of mud and decay upon them, moving to the monotonous rhythm of her task – shift down, move the blade forward, heave upwards once more. Her fingers, too, were caked and crusted with peat, not trim and clean as they had been when she and Murdo had danced beside that wall of stone and cement sheltering the sands curling round the coastline there.

There were others in the distance working at the same task: Iain Dubh, with his teenage son; old Alasdair and his wife, Bellag. Mostly, they all worked away in silence, saving words and breath for the task they had to complete if they were to stay warm and fed in winter; the result of their labours fuel for both their household fire and stove.

'It's the worst thing about living in a small place,' Seonaid declared. 'The way gossip and false stories go round.'

'Aye. Faster than the average rabbit runs.' Jessie was all too aware why Seonaid was conscious of that. When her first child, Ruaraidh, had been born some six weeks premature, a tale had spun round that she had been expecting before she was married. There had been tears in church a few days after she'd heard that, a babble of denials one morning when she stepped into the post office. Enraged, she had shouted at them, aware that a few of those who had been circulating that tale were standing near its counter, that Murdo was away at sea and could do nothing to help protect her from their tongues. Especially if there might be a little truth in their tales. Jessie was aware that Murdo had a reputation for the ladies, particularly when he was away in foreign ports. Mairead had mentioned that to her in one of their late-night conversations – that young father conforming to her own view of men as wanderers and philanderers, becoming involved with others while writing home to their sweethearts back on the island.

'And you don't have to do anything to merit these stories,' Seonaid continued, her pace of work gathering speed in her outrage. 'They get told regardless of what you do.'

'I know. There's a few that have been told about me in my time. That George and I, for instance, had a fight the day he left on the *Metagama*. That this is why I wasn't on the pier that evening. Why he doesn't write home – not to his family or to me. I've even heard that he disappeared with one of the Russian women on board.' She chuckled drily. 'That he's been living out in a small town in Alberta with her for years.'

'It's amazing how their tongues are always so precise.'

'Aye. It's a special skill they have. Both that and an ability to see across the prairies, into the distance there.'

'Was that why you started going to the moor so often, to get away from them?'

'Oh, who knows? It might even have started with my gran. She loved nothing more than being out on the moor in places like Airigh Choinnich. Took me with her from time to time. It was there she used to tell me stories: about the MacCodrums in North Uist, the people who were supposed to be descended from a seal and a man; about the Blue Men of the Minch. Tales like that.'

'Tell me about them. I'll pass the story onto Ruaraidh when I go home.'

'All right…'

She spoke about it, for all that it made her breathless each time she lifted up a turf, placing it on the wall of peat she had constructed there, one that the wind whistled through. Beside it there was a small gap of heather. Designed mainly to prevent those working from dirtying their shoulders, it was called *rathad an isein* – the birds' path. It often featured in Jessie's imagination – a trek where wrens and sparrows might walk, dancing on the edge of the bank.

'It's said that there are a race of blue men living in the Minch, not far from its surface. They're a wee bit like sharks or dolphins, bobbing up and down just below the waves, playing games, able even to talk to fishermen when they pass by on their boats. There are times, though, when they're just like the rest of us. They get mad and irritated by their neighbours, these men with whom they share the seas. They stir up storms, try to bring down their boats. Before they do this, they speak to them, reciting verses. If the fishermen are able to respond to them with rhymes, their boats are safe. If, however, they do not, they churn up the sea, sending their ships to the bottom, roaring with laughter as the boats capsize.'

And all the time she was saying these things, she was thinking to herself that if these Blue Men existed, they had every reason to be furious just now. They had seen that boat anchored in their waters, heard the chattering of monkeys, the scrambling of rats from inside its hold. They had watched, too, that spray rise up from the crest of waves, perhaps the wings of gulls being coated with the vapours. Their homes were being poisoned. The surface of the sea was being laid waste by the ship that had arrived there.

She looked up, hearing the cry of *an guilbneach,* the curlew, the movement of its flight encircling the sky above the moorland like the shape of a single teardrop, its cry imitating the sound of weeping. It was as if it was paying witness to all that was going on, that boat anchored out there between Tolsta and Cellar Head, the actions that those men in white suits were performing. With the emptiness of the moorland between her village and the tip of Ness, there were so few people who could note and observe what was going on that the bird had to provide its own testimony, its own record of what was occurring, that single sound of mourning the only proper and exact response.

There was no doubt about it. The earth was in need of healing, especially after what the men on that boat had done to God's creatures, those monkeys and the small, round rats.

12

Duncan was still angry when he reached home that night, going over the words of Eachainn in his head. What gave him the right to speak like that? Age? Grief? Loss? Sorrow? The fact that he had been away and out of the village for a few days? Why did he think it was fine to suggest another man was imagining things, especially since he had a witness, another person at his side? Why did he seem to believe that anyone – in this case – was telling lies or being some kind of traitor? Why didn't he accept that his fellow villager was speaking the truth?

It even irritated him that his mother was at home, having prepared supper for him. A couple of sausages and eggs. A few slices of bread. She was talking, too, about how the minister had announced in the midweek service that he intended to conduct a series of sermons about the plagues of Egypt.

'He'll start with the waters of the Nile being turned to blood, how the fish there died and the river stank, how blood was everywhere in the country. After that, he'll talk about the other plagues that God brought down on the heads of the people of Egypt.'

'That's interesting,' he muttered, aware that the minister's plague warnings were some of the constant themes of his mother's conversations, ever since she had been caught up in the religious revival that had occurred in the island over the last few years. His bus was filled with constant reminders of the changes over that time, the seats crammed with passengers who were travelling to church in some other district, Carloway, perhaps, Stornoway or Ness. He was even aware that sometimes they were praying for him as he drove to and from the town, seeking to ensure his soul was on a different direction to the one it was now taking – as one old man from the village of Vatisker had told him once.

'Oh, it is. It is,' his mother declared. 'The most amazing thing of all is what he told me at the end of the service. It had all been inspired by you, what you and Jessie found on the sands. He said that it might well be a sign, that the kingdom of heaven is on hand, that the end of the world may be coming.' She chuckled. 'That's interesting, isn't it? That what you found has inspired men of God to speak, to bring new souls to Him, that people see what you saw on that shoreline as a sign. Someday, you'll be a minister just like your cousin down in Lochs. Someday, the Lord will find the means to do that.'

This time he mumbled something indistinct in response. It's what irritated him most – this kindness. Her compliments, her judgements of him and his capabilities slipped sometimes into delusion. Her crazy belief, for instance, that he could ever become a minister. Just because he went to church with her twice every Sunday. Just because he kind of half-believed. Didn't she know that he lacked the patience to sit down and study? That books and paper were a mystery to him. That he solved the puzzles of life by examining an engine, slipping between the back wheels of a vehicle to find out if something was wrong with the workings of an exhaust. That he had been this way since he was a lad in his teens. It was for this reason the people of Tolsta valued him, appreciating an expertise that was still largely alien to them, with almost all of them still dependent on their horses to plough their fields and carry peats home. Why didn't she just accept that's who he was?

Yet he also knew she was undoubtedly one of the most pleasant-natured people in the village. Her grey hair and dark scarf, her black dress and jumper were continually glimpsed going in and out of people's doorways, delivering scones and pancakes for the people there to eat. 'I've made too much,' she would declare, 'I can never work out exactly what the right measurements are.' And so she'd hand out the excess, unaware that the people in these households had worked out exactly what she was doing, that she deliberately made more than she required for her own home. 'I feel like I'm drowning in flour,' one of their neighbours Donald Gunn had complained. 'It floods into the house every time your mother opens the door.'

There were times, too, when it wasn't only scones and pancakes. It might be peats she sneaked in the direction of others, when she noticed that someone's stack was becoming small. On other occasions, it might be a bag of potatoes, a chunk of mutton, a cluster of turnips. On most occasions, this was done secretly. Nobody else would be aware that it had happened.

He wondered when it had all started, this sympathy and open-heartedness that had almost become an embarrassment for him. There had been touches of it there even before his father had died, way back in 1945. The loan of a spade, which their neighbour would forget to return. A bucket or two of grain for hens someone in the village had neglected to buy for those that squawked and pecked around their home. And then there would be the reluctance to ask anyone to bring that item back. 'Do we need to? If they require it so desperately, can't we just leave it with them?' His father, never the most slim or slender of men, would increase in size and scale when she said something like that, his heels dancing up and down in frustration, his stomach swelling out. 'We can't allow people to take advantage of us,' he'd hiss. 'Word gets round.' It was true that just after her husband's passing, she had retreated into herself for a while. For all that her mourning did not make much sense to him, Duncan had come home from the war to find her in constant tears, her cheeks continually wet and stained for months afterwards. Slowly, though, she had shut the door against the dark, the weight and burden of clouds, and allowed the gleam of the lighthouses at Stoer and Cape Wrath across the Minch, Tiumpan Head, Stornoway, Butt of Lewis on the island, to find their way through the black that had long shrouded her. Sometimes these lights shone around the heights of the village like a loose, untidy web, wrapping and tangling round the houses.

Now there was this – the moments when he would step into the barn and byre and find something within its walls had gone. The other day it had been a scythe. He had wanted it to cut down a patch of old, dead grass and stubborn weeds he had neglected to hack away last year, looking forward to an hour or two swinging and chopping in the warmth of an early summer day. When he looked, however, there was no sign of it in its usual place.

'I think I gave it away,' she said.

'Who to?'

'I can't remember. Someone came round to the house, asking to borrow it.'

'And?'

'I've no idea who it was.'

He brooded for days after that – the tangle of grass and weeds a constant reminder to him of what she had done. She spent her time shuffling away from him, avoiding his company, even sometimes his gaze.

'Can you still not remember who you gave it to?'

She would shake her head.

'You're impossible.'

Eventually, she came up to him one evening, her face once again stained with the tears that had been constantly in evidence after his father's passing. 'Now, I know what you think,' she declared. 'That I'm a constant embarrassment to you. That I can't be relied on even to remember whom I've given things to. I'm sorry about that. Really sorry.'

He didn't say anything, unable to react.

'I wish I were gone from here. I know only too well that if I wasn't here, you'd be able to find a wife for yourself, someone with whom you could share your life. Remember, I…'

'Mam,' he interrupted.

'Let me continue' – she wagged her finger – 'Remember, I know what it's like to be a new wife coming into a house where there's already another woman in charge. When I married your father, his mother was always around – in charge of the kitchen, listening into our conversations, more even than that I daresay. I hated every moment of it. I wouldn't wish that situation on any other woman, least of all anyone that you chose to marry. You can understand that. Can't you?'

'Mam,' he spoke again, moving towards her to perform an act he hadn't performed since he was a child: giving her a hug.

'That's not the whole story. I just want you to be more careful with what we own, not giving things away without asking my permission. That's all I want you to do.'

'That's fine. I'll try to remember. I promise.'

Lying in his bed that night, he thought about what he had said to her. No. It wasn't the whole story, but it was undoubtedly part of it. When he sat near Ina in the Lido Café in the afternoon, he was aware that it was one of the reasons he felt unable to ask her out. He knew, though, there were many others. Even after his grandmother passed away, his father had been a silent, sullen man, rarely speaking to his own wife when they lived in the same house, only occasionally talking to him when he was a child. How could he know the right way to speak to a woman if he had an example like that? Wasn't it hard enough, without these things? But he knew, too, he didn't want to take Ina to a house in which his mother still lived. He had spoken to others about this from time to time, those who had spent the early years of their married life in a home where a shadow fell – whether deliberately or by accident – on their every conversation, where each single whisper might be overheard. Why should any young woman choose to put up with that? Weren't the early years of two people sharing a house together difficult and awkward enough without it?

And then there was something else he was beginning to recognise within himself: how his years at war had affected him. It was not just the memory of that explosion the time he drove past South Barrack Square, the memory of the blast that sometimes woke him up when he was sleeping. Nor was it the recollections of those he had seen dead or wounded in that conflict. No. There was more than that. He had become far too used to the company of men while he was in Gibraltar. There were few young women around with whom he could spend time, learn the tricks and ploys of talking to the opposite gender. He never felt entirely at ease when they were present. There was that moment in La Línea, one that came back to him again and again. Once, he had even felt sick and dizzy when he came across an officer in the Wrens sitting in a café in Casemates Square, watching – as he sometimes did when Ina was close – her legs as she crossed and uncrossed them, the nylon stockings she wore. He had stammered when she came near him, unable to speak.

An officer who had seen him had sidled up later, smiling as he spoke. 'You're suffering from Rockitis, I see?'

He hadn't got over that problem. He merely transferred his symptoms from one rock to another, his frailties staying with him when he reached home.

Where the hell would he ever find a cure?

Part Two

Fonn

– melody

Mhòrag Leat Shiùbhlainn

An uair a ghleusas i suas a h-òran
An uiseag thèid i na tosd 's an smeòrach,
'S iad ri èisteachd ceòl nèamhaidh rò-bhinn,
Ceòl binn gun euslan bho beul a'dòrtadh.

Morag, I Would Go With You

When she begins to sing,
the lark and thrush no longer chant or chirp,
listening to the music
note-perfect from her lips.

By Murdo Macfarlane – Murchadh MacPhàrlain

13

The sea closed in that morning, both mainland and island disappearing behind cloud and rain. A sharp wind set the gulls in motion. Reeling above the vessel, their shrieks had woken up John from his slumbers. Now up on deck he shivered, having experienced yet another troubled night of sleeplessness. Most of the men in his quarters had been playing cards or dominoes in the hours before, the kind of activities they often used to pass the time. Another one, Wilson, took a break from the piano in the ship's restaurant, practising instead the theme of *The Third Man* on his accordion, summoning visions of Ferris wheels and Viennese sewers, Orson Welles stepping from the shadows of a backstreet in Vienna. When he finished, a round of applause echoed, the vessel pitching to its side on an unexpected wave.

'I'll have to see if that works on the bagpipes sometime,' Mackay, the Scotsman, muttered.

The others groaned.

'Oh no,' Harvey laughed. 'Anything but that.'

However, John had not paid much attention to all that. Instead, he spoke to Lambert, listening to his stories about how his wife, Judith, was working as an English teacher somewhere outside Salisbury. She was constantly pressing books on him: recent novels, like *1984*, by a man called George Orwell; and more obscure titles like Boccaccio's *Decameron* and Chaucer's *Canterbury Tales* stacked below his bunk.

'The last I can barely make heads or tails of,' his friend grinned. 'Even though it's a modern translation.'

It was different with another book he had in his possession: *Poems*, by William Blake. Lambert kept pointing out lines he had underscored or noted with his pencil, prodding them with the tip of his finger.

A Robin Redbreast in a Cage
Puts all Heaven in a Rage.
A dove house fill'd with doves and pigeons
Shudders Hell thro' all its regions...
The bleat, the bark, bellow and roar
Are waves that beat on Heaven's shore...
Expect poison from the standing water...
Kill not the Moth nor Butterfly
For the Last Judgment draweth nigh...

'I think she was trying to tell me that the work we are doing here is wrong. She's very good at that, hinting but never saying, correcting me in her own sweet way. I think that's what she was doing here by giving me these books, trying to make me think for myself. What do you reckon?'

'I don't know her. I can't comment.'

'But what do you think?' Lambert repeated.

John shrugged, unable to answer. 'I think only you can respond to that. Only you know her well enough.'

All the time, he was thinking that Lillian hadn't been as subtle as that. He recalled the way she had come into the Old Oak Inn a few months after they had arrived in Salisbury. Her face dark and serious, she sank into the seat beside him. For once, she was silent, withdrawing into herself in a way she had never done while working in the Talbot Inn back home.

'You all right?' he asked.

She shook her head.

'What's the matter?

'Get me a gin and tonic and I'll tell you.'

'Oh, I was just about to do that anyway. Give me a minute.'

A moment or two later and he set the glasses down before them. 'Well?'

'I thought you told me your job was something like a vet,' she said. 'That's what you told me up in Liverpool. Some sort of drivel about enzymes and their effect upon animals. It isn't, is it?'

'It's part of it.'

'But it's not all. Is it?'

'No. Sometimes we try and develop cures for certain diseases, testing them out on certain animals.'

'And?'

He shifted in his seat, irritated by her questioning. 'I can't talk about some things I do at work. I signed the Official Secrets Act.'

'Oh, piffle!' She rocked back her head and laughed. 'Oh, that's no excuse! I bet most men who work there don't pay too much attention to that kind of thing. They whisper all sorts of secrets to their wives in bed. Probably to others, too.'

'Well, we're not at home at the moment,' he mumbled, looking at all the faces that were swirling round him in the pub. One of them – a man who spent much of his time in the Old Oak writing letters to the local newspaper – was even approaching them, just to tell Lillian about some squabble or other he was having with his neighbours, asking her to examine his latest epistle before he placed it in the post. She indulged him in the same way she had once done with Billy the Lip, nodding her head at his every remark, her wide smile gleaming. Afterwards, she would abandon her pretence, turning to him and frowning.

'What an utter bore that man is!'

It occurred to him – not for the first time – what an excellent spy Lillian would make. Again and again she demonstrated an astonishing ability to conceal her true feelings behind a grin or glazed expression, belonging completely in any room she stepped within. She could manipulate, too. Time and time again he had seen this. The old men in the Talbot squeezing cash into her hand. Those whose gaze followed her, watching her every move. He jolted himself with the thought that this was exactly the kind of person they had warned him about in the security meetings he had attended in Sutton Oak and Porton Down: 'Watch out for the chameleons, the ones that can charm and win people over. The ones you trust most – your wife or neighbour, your best friend. Those you find attractive. Those who question you about the nature of your work.'

He slammed the thought from his head, aware of how ridiculous it sounded, even to his own mind. Lillian was not a spy. She came from a fishing family in Fleetwood. Conservative-minded. Churchill supporters. Deeply Christian. Little interest in politics. Just an ordinary young woman who loved children and animals. She would often pat and frisk people's dogs when they went on a walk together – labradors, collies, Pekinese, any that came near their path. She had a real talent at getting on with others.

He shook himself, trembling in the chill of the wind. He had to stop thinking of her like that, pay attention instead to his job. Today, it was his task to stand on the deck with binoculars in hand, alongside one of the many rusty cauldrons found dangling around the vessel. Drawings of the cauldrons – sketched by Parker, an earnest, bespectacled man who worked alongside John in the laboratory – were pinned up on the various notice-boards on the ship. One showed Stalin with his broad smile and moustache, sitting inside a cauldron. Another had a caricature of a Chinese man in a cauldron waving a red flag. Yet another showed steam rising from a hammer and sickle stuffed within a pot – a monkey or goat grinning over its brim. John caught himself smiling each time he noticed a new drawing appear.

'It's just a little joke,' Shepherd had said, nodding towards one when they first joined the ship. 'With work like this, we've got to find ways of keeping our spirits up. All part of the brew.'

'At least they're a bit more cheerful than some of the other posters on view,' Lambert said dryly later, nodding towards the *Classified* posters also pinned to the noticeboards. 'They always bring a broad smile to my face.'

John grinned weakly. These posters informed the men of some of the symptoms of the gases that were being used on board:

Tularemia – otherwise known as rabbit or fly fever – easy to contaminate – causing fever, skin ulcers, enlarged lymph nodes.

Brucellosis – also known as Malta or Mediterranean fever – causing fevers, stomach problems including nausea.

Bubonic plague – like pneumonic plague caused by the bacterium Yersina pestitis *– causing fever, headaches, vomiting, death within ten days.*

As with most of the other men, John's eyes would skirt over the information. At some level, he just didn't want to know what he was dealing with each morning. Visions of it crept into his dreams often enough at night.

As preparations were being made for today's testing, there were more men watching from the deck than before, as a result of what had happened a few days before. Some of the youngsters from the village had dived into the sea from the edge of the beach. Wilson, the accordionist, hadn't noticed them clustering there – too busy imagining, perhaps, that the rhythm of the sea was not unlike that of his favourite instruments as it rocked the boat from side to side. Only at the last moment, as the flag was being raised, the red light shown, the warning blast just about to be sounded, did he become aware that he could hear a scream of laughter, see the flash of arms and legs. He froze for a moment.

'Help! There are lads out there!'

They stopped things just in time. No explosion. No wave of gas. No bubonic plague drifting on the breeze towards those young lads. Instead, one of the motorboats set off in their direction. Those on board warned the local youngsters about the hazards of what they were doing, how they should watch out for the red flag being raised, how they were putting their lives in danger.

'Get out of here now!' they yelled back. 'Go home!'

'Thalla dhachaigh!' Mackay shouted, using the few words of Gaelic he knew. And then there were the muttered words of explanation: 'We're doing this for you, you know! We're doing this for you!'

But that didn't happen today. Instead, just as the trail of

gas rose and puffed out from the pontoon, one of those on guard spotted something coming out of the veil of mist and rain towards him.

'Stop it! Stop it!' he shouted.

John lifted his binoculars to look in the direction the man was pointing. There was a fishing boat there, the name *Carella* painted in white letters on its black bow. Scanning down, he noticed the boat's number, *FD258*, just below the name. 'Fleetwood,' he thought to himself – and Lillian was in his head again. Was one of her relatives on board that boat? John imagined him meeting her, shaking her hand or giving her a brief hug, perhaps, as they met in Station Road or Jubilee Gardens, looked out on Morecambe Bay. During that moment, the poison might be transported – brucellosis, tularemia, bubonic or pneumonic plague travelling from one person to another like a parcel being passed, the choking of breath, chest pains, vomiting, the inevitability of death. He shivered as he thought of it, picturing the horror in his mind as he watched the vessel continue its voyage, cutting through the halo of gas spilling on the surface of the sea.

'Stop! Stop! Stop!' he yelled.

He wasn't the only one behaving like that. They all were. Some were hollering; others sounding alarms, flashing lights, striking the railings with whatever they could clutch or bang. The monkeys were chattering, the guinea pigs chirruping. Even the gulls seemed to be joining in, these carriers of pestilence and plague winging their way around the *Carella*'s decks, adding their own harsh metallic voices to the uproar.

Using his binoculars, John struck the cauldron hanging nearby, doing it time and time again. As he did so, a thousand visions came to mind. Victoria Pier in Fleetwood lined with corpses, laid out beside one another. The copper birds on top of the Liver Building looking down on the dead lining Liverpool's streets. The Ferris wheel – or some such – in Blackpool stalling, unable to stir because of the load it had to bear. The theme of *The Third Man* transformed…

Yet, despite their noise and uproar, the *Carella* continued southwards through the Minch, making its way towards Broadbay and the peninsula of Point, past sand and shingle, skerries and rocks, small islands and fishing ports, as it sailed with a hold filled with cod caught in Icelandic waters in the direction of home.

14

For all that it was raining, Jessie was singing to herself –
something she had not done for ages – as she made her way
across the moor, the words of *Eilean Beag Donn a' Chuain*,
that song she and Mairead used to sing together in the years
after the *Metagama* sailed from Stornoway, the one they had
learned from the singing teacher at school. Despite the gloom
of its words, its recollections of the First World War, it came
to her lips in a cheerful way, the lilt of its rhythm accompanying her steps as she made her way around streams, lochs
and bogland, collecting plants and flowers and placing them
in the sack she carried.

Do làmh, a charaid, gu Eilean a' chuain
'S a h-eallach cho chruidh is trom,
Tha'm bàs na chabhaig, ri sgathadh 's a' buain,
gun duine nì suas an call;
Tha'n òigridh sgoinneil a sheòlas na caoil
an àite nan laoich a bh'ann,
Gun bhoineid gun bròig a' siubhal nan raon
an Eilean an Fhraoich ud thall.

Your hand, my friend, for that sea-circled isle
With its burden borne at great cost,
Where death in its hurry cuts and harvests,

And no one to make up the loss;
The active youths who sail the narrows
in place of the heroes that were,
Without hat, without shoes, travelling the fields
On the Island of Heather out there.

It was mainly *lus nan laogh*, or bog-bean, that she gathered near the edge of lochs. The trick was to pull the plants out by the roots shortly after their white, feathery flowers had died away, their fruits having formed. After this, they would be cleansed and boiled, simmering away for a couple of hours in a pan before the liquid was squeezed, strained and bottled. A number of people took this in the village, believing it cured all their ills and ailments. Some would even hold their noses as they swallowed the potion, gulping as they swigged it down.

'It's a lot better than pills from Dr Gillies or Dr Macaulay. Much, much better.'

'Goodness knows what might happen if their medicines ever stopped working – and we've forgotten all about what we've used for centuries before.'

There were other plants too she lifted as she walked along. The yellow flowers of tormentil that sometimes gleamed alongside a peat-track. She had heard this called by two names, *braonan fraoich* or *braonan-a'-mhadaidh-ruaidh*. She preferred the second name, summoning up visions of the fox for her, prowling the borders of North Tolsta, its eye perhaps on the sheep that grazed there, rather than a reminder of the heather that was all around her. It was used when someone was suffering diarrhea. And then there was St John's wort, *achlasan Chaluim Chille*, to cheer people up when they felt miserable and low. Occasionally, in patches of green, there was self-heal growing, *lus-a-chridhe*, which – despite its name – was good for sore throats and wounds. She loved the way, too, that both weather and season played with their shades, mixing and mingling, changing the moor's hues from brown to green, sometimes sprinkling other colours within its length and breadth.

She plucked these plants, occasionally sipping water from a stream she knew ran fresh and clear, bending down to cup it in her palm. All the time she was conscious of the birds around her, their flight attending each stride of her walk. She could see a group of ravens picking away at something at the edge of a loch, watched by a seagull that followed their every move. For a moment, she wondered if they might have swooped down on another monkey or tubby little rat swept in on the tide, tearing at flesh till bone is exposed, but she shook her head, chasing the thought from her head. Instead, she glanced at a curlew a short distance away, probing peat or mud before tugging out its prey with a wriggle of its bill. There was also a heron standing in Loch Langabhat, upright and wary. From time to time it appeared to gaze in her direction in a maniacal way, its yellow eyes glaring, as if it were one of those busybodies from the village, watching everybody else's moves.

It wasn't, however, these things that had made her go out to the moor in the first place. It wasn't even the need to get away from the eyes of people – though that undoubtedly played a part. No. Sometimes, it was the way she kept believing she saw George among the familiar surroundings of the village. She glimpsed him sometimes in the school playground, in the form of some fair-haired boy who was one of his distant relatives, recognising the same shape or form, the blue-eyed intensity of his gaze. At other times, she might hear his voice, some man cursing a horse he was finding hard to control as he ploughed a field, another singing a song from Skye that had been a familiar sound on his lips, especially in the weeks before he was set to journey on the *Metagama*.

An tèid thu leam, a rìbhinn òg,
A rìbhinn òg, a rìbhinn òg,
An tèid thu leam, a rìbhinn òg,
A-null gu tìr nam beanntan?

Will you go with me, my young maid,
My young maid, my young maid,
Will you go with me, my young maid
Over to the land of mountain?

And then there was the time she saw the young men diving from rocks into the sea on the village shoreline. One of them emerged with his fair hair tight against his head, his strong, muscular body glistening with water. She saw a few wisps of hair in the youth's armpits, one or two beginning to appear on his chest, the breadth of his shoulders and his tight, taut backside, and she felt something stir within herself she had not sensed for a long time, the remnants of a feeling long forgotten for a man who had, over time, been transformed into a ghost. He might be occasionally glimpsed too in the post office, on the pier, stepping from a cave the sea had long ago ground through the base of a tower of rock on Garry Sands; a spirit that still haunted the village road, though – miraculously, mysteriously – never appeared on the moorland. Gritting her teeth, she would move away, resolving never to look in that direction again.

As the rain began to lash, Jessie cut short her walk, heading back towards the village. No matter what the day was like, however, she always made a short detour towards the Tràigh Mhòr. There was always something different on view there. In winter, it might be snow, edging little lines of lace on the sand, blinding the cattle caught in an unexpected shower on the machair. Once or twice, it had been an old dog one of the local crofters had drowned, a sack filled with kittens someone else had thrown from a cliff. One day, she even found a minke whale washed up on the beach, lost and disorientated, drowning in air, wondering, perhaps, why it was no longer swimming in the shallow waters of the Minch. Soon, the small figures of crofters and their families began to mill around it, anticipating meat for the coming of winter, oil for their lamps, bones they could employ, say, to weigh their hay-stacks down, preventing the wind from gusting away each strand. Shortly after they were gone, the people of the village were replaced by a gathering of gulls, anxious to pluck the stranded mammal clean of flesh.

It was as she approached Tràigh Mhòr that she heard the commotion. The clamour of voices. The sounding of alarms. Bell being clanged and struck. A hoot or two. She raced down to the machair to look, running into the force of the wind. When she got there, she saw a large trawler, bigger than any of the local boats, sailing down the Minch, its crew either deaf or ignoring all evidence of the disturbance its presence among them had caused, sailing on and on through the cursing and the noise.

15

Duncan's head was full of voices when he parked the bus outside his home that night. It had been a busy day. In the Lido, his friend, Roddy George had been ranting about rationing, how its end was long overdue.

'It's been years since the war finished. Isn't it time to start enjoying as many cups of tea as we'd like? Bloody Labour government. Trying to even out the misery. It made that go on and on.'

Another of his companions, Iain from Carloway, had talked about how there was going to be a football match in Goathill Park soon, between Inverness Caley and the Lewis Select.

'Something to look forward to,' Iain said. 'Especially when there's so few teams playing in the League this year. There's even going to be a dance in the Town Hall afterwards.'

'That'll be good,' Duncan grinned. 'Do you know who's playing?'

'No idea… Probably the Stornoway Dance Band.'

And then they had spoken about the *Ben Lomond*, how most of them felt that the government was quite right undertaking tests like these.

'We've got to protect ourselves from the Russkies.'

'We've no idea what they might be up to. Stalin's a pretty ruthless bastard. Worse than any of our lot.'

It was in the middle of this talk that Ina had entered the café.

Duncan saw her through the spin and eddy of tobacco smoke, the constant blur that dimmed and blurred the Lido's cream-coloured walls, for all that they had been freshly painted a few weeks before. Someone had said that it sometimes looked like the inside of one of the old blackhouses on the islands, with a swirl of peatsmoke rising and falling within its walls, obscuring chairs and tables with its mist. Duncan held his breath as he watched her, noting the steadiness and grace of her approach, how neat and trim she was. As she made her way towards him, his heart drummed faster than he could ever recall it doing before.

'My boss was wondering if you could do us a favour,' she said.

'Yes. Of course. Of course,' he stammered.

'Some of the tweeds we sent out were short of a few spools of wool. Could you deliver them to the weavers in Back or Tolsta? They'll meet the bus as usual.'

'Of course,' he mumbled again.

'That'll be good. My boss will be grateful.'

'That's all right.'

She turned on her heel, going to Luigi at the counter to order her coffee. The Italian was clearly comfortable in her company, cheerful and joking as they stood there. She was one of the regular customers in the place, perhaps someone with whom he decided to risk a word or two of Gaelic, testing out his knowledge of the tongue. It was then Duncan decided to speak again, waiting until the sound of their voices fell away.

'You going to the dance that's on soon?' he asked.

'Which one?'

'The one in the Town Hall in a few weeks' time. After the football match.'

'I might,' she said as she paid for her drink. 'If someone asks me.'

'Well, I'm asking.'

'I'll probably go then,' she grinned.

'Good.'

And his friends Roddy George and Iain laughed, nudging him with their elbows, winking in his direction.

His head had been in turmoil ever since that moment, a thousand questions tumbling through his thoughts. They had bewitched, bothered and bewildered him every inch of the road home, each time he stopped to deliver wool to weavers in the village for their tweeds. Did Ina really mean what she appeared to be saying? What if she was teasing and tormenting him? If she was serious, what could he do about his mother? Where could she go to? Would she stay with them? How could they manage?

And now, just as he stepped out of his bus, there was Jessie waiting for him, shivering and damp, wrapped in her thick coat.

'Guess what happened out there today,' she said.

'Sorry?'

'Out near Tolsta Head. The boat... A fishing boat went past. Just when they were testing something. That spray thing we've noticed before. The explosion...'

'Yes?'

'A fishing boat went past. There was a lot of shouting. Panicking. Yelling. Alarms going off. Something was clearly very wrong.'

'A fishing boat from here?'

'No. One from England somewhere. Or somewhere down south.'

He shrugged his shoulders. He didn't quite know how to respond to Jessie, what to do now this had happened – if indeed it really had. He knew he had become tired thinking about the subject, especially now he had other questions to occupy his mind. There had been too many conversations about this ship just outside the Tràigh Mhòr. Too many people had given different advice. Besides, what could either he or Jessie do about the situation? Write a letter to Macmillan, the MP? Speak to a councillor? Scribble a note and send it to 10 Downing Street or the readers' page of the *Stornoway Gazette*? These days he felt a little like he had sometimes done while he had been in Gibraltar: strafed on all sides, caught in a cross of searchlights, aware that the lights in the buildings all around them were switched on in the forlorn hope that they might be mistaken for neutral Spain across the border – for all that the situation he was now in was a little less deadly than it had been back then.

'You don't know exactly where down south?'

'No.'

'Or the fishing boat's name?'

'No. It was too far away.'

'Well, where do we start then? Where do we start?' He shrugged his shoulders and turned away in the darkness before halting a few moments later, halfway to his back door. 'We'll have to leave those onboard the boat to handle things. We've little choice about that.'

16

'We've decided what we're going to do about yesterday,' Shepherd said to the men gathered on the deck.

After a night in hell, and a wet and blustery day out of kilter with the season, the sun had been restored. Despite its warmth, John felt cold and chilled. Dreams and nightmares had dragged him out of sleep time and time again during the mix of dark and twilight that had filled the hours before – just as they had done for many nights before. He had tussled with his thoughts – hearing Tolbin one moment, Lillian or Lambert the next – moaning and trying to kick their words away, so much so that Mackay the Scotsman in the bunk two or three away from where he lay had growled at him.

'Will you shut up? Will you shut the hell up?'

'I'm sorry,' he whispered, shutting his eyes.

Moments later, however, he was awake again – Lillian exploding into his thoughts. He remembered how they had quarrelled when she finally discovered the nature of his work. Those days she'd spent in Emmanuel United Church came to the fore: she had muttered continually about how mankind had 'a covenant with the animals', that we had a duty to care for them and not exploit or misuse them in any way. When he asked what she meant by that, she hauled out an old King James Bible from the top of the wardrobe, pointing out a verse from the book of Hosea.

And in that day will I make a covenant for them with

*the beasts of the field and with the fowls of heaven, and
with the creeping things of the ground: and I will break the
bow and the sword and the battle out of the earth, and will
make them to lie down safely.*

'There's a lot more where that came from,' she muttered,
'You're crossing a line by doing these things to animals. You're
crossing a line. We've no right to behave like that to them.'

He shrugged when she said this, unable to counter her
argument, a side of her that he had never seen before.

'I remember a preacher coming to Fleetwood when I was
young,' she said. 'He talked about how important it was to look
after the least of God's creatures, how the way we treated them
was a measure of both a man's faith and his kindness, that no
man could be considered a man of God if he mistreated the
beasts of the field. Unlike so many others who climbed into that
pulpit, his words made a huge impression on me. It seemed
to me that he was right.' She paused for a moment, drawing
breath. 'Tell you what, John Herrod, how do you think you
stand in that equation? Do you think you're doing right?'

Again he shrugged. 'I do what I'm paid to do.'

'And that makes it right?'

'It isn't quite as simple as you make out. What we do saves
lives sometimes.'

'At what cost to the existence of other beings on this planet?
The monkey? The guinea pig? The mouse?'

One more shrug. One more muttered remark: 'I do what I
do to get by.'

'That's not good enough. That's not good enough at all.'

It was this that had brought about her leaving when he said

he was about to go somewhere to take part in animal testing.

'I can't tell you where,' he muttered. 'It would be against the Official Secrets Act if I did.'

'You and your flaming Official Secrets Act!' she spat in his direction. 'You know what I'm going to do? I'm going to back to Fleetwood when you're away, spend time with Mum and Dad, my brothers and sisters. If you're serious about keeping this marriage alive, you know what you'll have to do. Leave Porton Down. I've heard stories about the terrible things that happen at that place. Men scorched or blinded by the tests they do there. Animals killed and slaughtered. Why don't you give up this job! You can come up to Fleetwood and get me if you decide to do that.'

These had been among her last words to him as he packed his suitcase to travel to the *Ben Lomond,* to take part in Operation Cauldron. They had repeated, too, in his head almost from the instant he had watched the *Carella* sail through the haze of spray set off on the pontoon, mingling, perhaps, a shipload of bubonic plague together with cod fished from the waters close to Iceland. John could imagine hell let loose in the boat's home-port of Fleetwood, free and unconfined, uncoiling like the rope the fishermen threw out to fasten their vessel to the pier, spiralling round the town's streets, encircling its lighthouses, going from hand to hand, face to face, breath to breath, an invisible mist that seeped through the open windows of houses, crept unseen across the threshold of people's homes.

And he could see Lillian, too, playing her own part in passing that plague to others, squeezing up close to the likes of Billy the Lip at the bar, ruffling someone's dog with her fingers, kissing that dark-haired stranger he always imagined her to be with. It seemed to him that his eyes opened wider in darkness, envisaging these sights. It was daylight that hid truth from him, obscuring and making invisible the horrors that were all around.

Standing now on the *Ben Lomond*'s deck, John slammed his fist and palm together, trying to chase all these thoughts away. Instead, he concentrated on Shepherd's words, their weight at odds with his youthful-looking face. He was talking about how they didn't know why no one on board the *Carella* had responded to the flags and clamour that surrounded the boat when it sailed into the area.

'It's as if she had turned into the *Mary Celeste...*'

Shepherd became more serious after that, his voice deepening as he strove to put his message across.

'Clearly, however, it's left us with problems. At the most basic level, the captain will receive a reprimand for what has happened, taking the blame for the rest of us not being sufficiently vigilant and failing to check what's coming towards us on the horizon. Worse than that, there is the possibility the men on board that ship can pass this onto others, all across the north of England and beyond. It's why we've had to contact the government about what happened. No less a person than Winston Churchill, the Prime Minister himself. They've decided to allow the boat entry into Fleetwood harbour with the following precautions taking place. The crew will be followed wherever they go, both within the town of Fleetwood and beyond. Every time they step on a bus or train, they will be watched. On every occasion they go to a home or foreign harbour, their movements will be followed. And this will happen for a long, long time. Months, if not years. Their medical records, too, will be carefully checked for signs or symptoms that the bubonic plague has passed onto them. And the latter will also be the case for all their relatives and family, everyone with whom they come into contact on a daily basis. That is what the government has decided. God help us if it all goes wrong.'

John felt himself grow weak again. He was forced to clutch the ship's railings in order to keep upright, focusing on the movement of a cauldron as the vessel pitched from side to side.

17

Finlay the postman scooped out a letter from his bag and handed it to Jessie.

'There's an interesting stamp on it,' he declared. 'Would you mind keeping it and giving it to me later? It's for my son. He collects these things.'

'Of course,' Jessie smiled, looking at it. A United States stamp, it bore a small sketch and the words *1452–1952: 500th Anniversary of the printing of the first book, The Holy Bible, from movable type, by Johann Gutenberg*. She knew right away that the letter was from Neil in Vermont, his handwriting on the envelope. She took a while before she read it, waiting until Finlay had clattered away on his bicycle before she did so.

Dear Jessie,

It's been a while since I wrote to you. There are many reasons for this. My wife Marianne died two months ago of a heart attack and I'm now on my own. I miss her dreadfully. She was a good friend and companion to me during much of our lives together, though in the last few years things grew difficult. She felt the strain of living in a place to which she did not belong. My friend Jock has suggested that I go home for a bit, visit eilean beag donn a' chuain and my brother and mother in Coll. Also my wife's people in Irvine. Some of them I've never met before, though I've heard so much about them. It's about time I got to know them all.

I think he's right. It's what I need at the moment, to catch up with those I know and love. Also see the places I've missed so much since I came out here on the Metagama all these years ago. What do you think? If I did, it would be great to meet up. We could catch up with one another in Stornoway. Someone has told me there's even Italian cafés there these days. What do you think? If you want, you can take me round Tolsta. As you know, I've got cousins there. I could go and see them when I'm in the village.

Let me know over the next few weeks. You don't have to write to me at my home address here in Vermont. Just send the letter care of my family in Coll. They'll pass it onto me when I arrive.

Hoping you are all well.

Best

Neil

That song was once again on her lips as she sat down to write her reply, the one about how much the community had been wounded and broken by the First World War.

A Dhia bi maille ri muinntir a' bhròin
'S na fir a tha leòinte, tinn,
Bho ìnean guineach na h-iolair' a bhòc
Air fuil agus feòil do chloinn;
Tha gaoth an fhir-mhillidh na itean; 's a chròg
A' dhruidheadh ma sgòrnan teann,
Tha 'n leòmhann a' fàsgadh Uilleam a Dhà
Is spiollaidh i chnàmhan lom.

Fonn

O God protect the sorrowful souls
And the men who are tired and suffering,
From the slash of the eagle, his body swelled up
With the flesh and gore of our offspring;
But devastation dishevels his feathers
And fingers clamp tight round his throat,
As the British lion crushes the Kaiser,
Preparing for that last onslaught.

18

All the way between Stornoway and Gress, Duncan had listened to two women sitting in the front passenger seat behind him, talking about Queen Elizabeth's coming coronation, their words punctuating every twist in the road, every turn of the wheel.

'It's going to be sometime next year,' Morag Morrison declared. 'And I've heard it's going to be on the wireless.'

'It would be almost worth going to London to see the whole thing,' her companion, Catriona, said. 'I've got a cousin down there. She's always asking me to go down and stay with her for a week or two.'

'It would cost a fortune.'

'Aye. That might be so. But it would be worth it. She's a young woman. It might be a very long time till the next one. I don't suppose we'll ever get the chance to see the like of it again. What with all the bands playing. The streets being full of people. It'll be amazing.'

'Aye. There's no doubt about that. But it would take a big chunk out of your pension. Besides, Stornoway is far enough away for me these days. And busy enough. They come from all over the island to be there. Even places like Buckie and Peterhead. I was standing beside one of their fishermen and, you know, I never understood a word they said.'

'That's not surprising. It's like a different language...'

His head reeled with all their chatter. Why couldn't they be quiet for a moment? Why couldn't they stay on the same subject? One minute they were talking about Prince Philip and the young Queen. The next they were speaking about their times gutting herring in the fishing ports of the East Coast, from Wick all the way down to Lowestoft and Great Yarmouth.

Duncan tried to keep his concentration on the road, but he also kept thinking about his mother. She belonged with the two women on the bus. Same age. Same love of faith and church. Same history, even of following the herring in her younger days. Yet in some ways, she was very different. Her charity, for instance. Was there a reason she was so kind to her neighbours? Was that her way of gaining love and attention from people? He knew she had never gained any of that from his father – a cold and distant man who rarely spoke either in his home or outside its walls. He could only recall the occasional grunt and mutter, a word or two squeezed from his pursed lips. Duncan remembered one of the village boys telling him in the school playground that the man with whom he shared his home wasn't his real dad – that his mother had given birth to him long before they were married.

'What?' he stammered. 'Is that true?'

He had never asked his mother or father if it ever was, frightened for many years that he might lose her love if he opened his mouth and uttered the question. It was only in the last few years that it had stopped troubling him. Perhaps it was better not to know.

Duncan usually slept well, but he didn't that night. Memories crowded in. There was that time in La Línea when the others persuaded him to join them. He was barely there two minutes and questions were cramming his head. Why on earth had he agreed to come with them? What had made him so stupid? The place was utterly depressing, its streets crammed with the shadows of the civil war that had taken place a few years before. There was a shanty town on the edge of La Línea, its buildings crammed and rickety, looking as if they could blow down in a breeze, reminding him for a moment of Lewis – the tents near the Blackwater where the tinkers stayed. The roads were filled with potholes; the lorry shuddering as it travelled along. The drains stank. Children in rags stretched out their hands and shouted '*Peniques*' in their direction, standing in their path as they walked along. And then there were the prostitutes themselves, some dressed in black and wearing mantillas on their heads, nervously speaking in a mix of Andalusian Spanish and poor English. Only two words were in any way decipherable to him.

'Good time… Good time…'

The woman he chose was even more nervous than himself. Shy, nervous, smelling of garlic, looking thin and exhausted, she pointed out the ring on her finger as she babbled something, somehow managing to tell him that her husband was either killed or missing. Perhaps he had been shot in the civil war. A lot of men around these parts had. Maybe he had disappeared into the woods or hills to escape Franco and his guards. She started trembling and crying, unable to stay still when he put his arms around her, half-drawing him towards her, half-pushing him away. Eventually, he pushed himself away, squeezing some coins into her hand.

'*Gracias*,' she muttered. '*Gracias*.'

He vomited a moment later, overwhelmed by that encounter, the smell within those streets.

It wasn't the only thing that made him sick about Gibraltar. There was the fear that haunted the place, cloaking those who lived there like the Levant cloud that draped the rock for days on end. It filled people with dread, the thought that the day would soon come when all its streets and battlements might suffer the same fate as those in Malta. Each day, the Germans and Italians appeared to be attempting to level that island, bombing the Grand Harbour of Valletta, rendering Kingsway into rubble, sinking the ships that tried to bring supplies to those stationed there. Occasionally, the men whispered to one another about what was happening and wondered when it might occur to them.

'We're next,' they predicted. 'After Malta, we're flaming next.'

There was also the way those who came across the border each day were treated, the Spaniards from La Línea who were employed around the Rock. They gained little thanks for their efforts, only snide remarks about the *hombre* who did most of the work about the place, the quality of the food they ate, their crude, uncouth ways. There was, too, the contempt with which some of the officers treated the lower ranks, how they sipped tea and looked down on ordinary men like him from their tiny, cramped flats in Castle Steps and Hampton Ramp.

The hell with them. What entitled them to treat people this way?

Among a thousand other reasons, it was this that had made him long to return to Tolsta. They treated people with decency here, no matter what they were like. They didn't feel the need to pass over money to a woman to imitate an act of love. They didn't even foul their minds with thoughts like that. Most of the time there was no fear of others, just an occasional awareness that there were some who were harsh and severe in their judgements, condemning others for one action or another.

In the darkness, the muted glow of a lamp, Duncan stretched out for the Bible, reading the section of the Scriptures that, according to his mother, the minister had spoken about that night.

1. Then the Lord said unto Moses, Go in unto Pharaoh, and tell him, Thus saith the Lord God of the Hebrews, Let my people go, that they may serve me.

2. For if thou refuse to let them go, and wilt hold them still,

3. Behold, the hand of the Lord is upon thy cattle which is in the field, upon the horses, upon the asses, upon the camels, upon the oxen, and upon the sheep: there shall be a very grievous murrain.

4. And the Lord shall sever between the cattle of Israel and the cattle of Egypt: and there shall nothing die of all that is the children's of Israel.

5. And the Lord appointed a set time, saying, Tomorrow the Lord shall do this thing in the land.

6. And the Lord did that thing on the morrow, and all the cattle of Egypt died: but of the cattle of the children of Israel died not one.

7. And Pharaoh sent, and, behold, there was not one of the cattle of the Israelites dead. And the heart of Pharaoh was hardened, and he did not let the people go.

As he read these words, he again became restless, thinking of the conversation he had with Finlay John on Stornoway quay, how the cattle in Aultbea had become poisoned with anthrax, lying dead among the grass; how, too, there were cattle grazing on the machair here. Could they too become infected with the trail of gas blowing in from the pontoon? He determined not to think about it, aware of only one thing.

It had been a mistake to choose to read from that part of the Bible tonight.

19

'It's our job to be the performing monkeys tonight,' Lambert declared when the whole crew gathered for the party. 'The chimpanzees at the tea party. All in our best bib and tucker to greet the visiting bigwigs. The PG Tips family out for lunch.'

'The Mr Shifters of Stornoway.' Parker's eyes sparkled in the direction of the dignitaries who had just come to the *Ben Lomond* for dinner, arriving at the vessel on a small motor boat. 'The Hebridean headmen are here.'

'The greatest shysters the town could provide,' Lambert grinned.

'Washed up on the incoming tide.'

'Flotsam on the beach.'

John barely listened to them. Lillian was back in his head once again, the way she always appeared when there was smoke swirling, drink passed around – reminding him of those days and nights when she was working in the Talbot Inn or relaxing in the Hermitage or Lime View, laughter tinkling like the glass she lifted again and again to her lips.

Earlier, Lambert had been talking again about his wife, Judith, and her habit of quoting Blake at him in the hope it might persuade him to leave his work. She had read out a section to him one particular night, telling him how:

Cruelty has a Human Heart
And Jealousy a Human Face
Terror the Human Form Divine
And Secrecy, the Human Dress

The Human Dress, is forged Iron
The Human Form, a fiery Forge.
The Human Face, a Furnace seal'd
The Human Heart, its hungry Gorge.

Despite himself, John felt the poet's words deeply. Most of them were true. He felt it in his bones each time he tried to communicate with Lillian about the work he was doing. Again and again, he had blurred some facts about his employment and revealed others, trying to tell her that much of the work they did in Porton Down was for human good, developing cures against illnesses, preparing the country's defences against any pandemics that might sweep in their direction, finding ways of preventing illnesses and disease. He had even informed her that they sometimes worked to protect domestic animals, such as cattle, chickens, sheep or pigs from the encroachment of other wild beasts, such as foxes, weasels and badgers from causing them harm or damage.

'It's important to protect the livelihood of farmers.'

'How do you do that?' she quizzed him.

He hesitated before telling her. 'We inject eggs with poison and leave them scattered around the outbuildings of farms. It's a fast and humane way of doing it – these wild animals coming to eat the eggs instead of preying on the farm animals.'

'Really? You do that?' Her eyes were wide with horror.

'Yes. It's better than allowing farmers, especially those with meagre incomes, to starve. For their animals to be attacked.'

'Pissshaw! That's utter nonsense! How can you believe that? How can you accept those kind of things could ever remotely be justified?'

And she kept returning to one small aspect of his work, reminding him about it time and time again. He would do his best to respond.

'We know that the Russians are ahead of us in nerve gas,' he told her, conscious he was breaking the Official Secrets Act as he did so. 'They took over a German factory in Silesia in the war, the place where they developed sarin and tabun. Three thousand tons of the stuff every month. We've got to protect ourselves from that. Make sure we can catch up and protect ourselves from everything they're doing.' He shook his head. 'If you but knew, there's so many things they're developing. Phosgene. Lewisite. White phosphorous. Mustard gas. Carbonyl Iron. Tear gas. And we've got to find ways of dealing with all of them.'

But, despite his arguments, she never relented, never gave in. *If we're going to have any future together, you've got to change your job*, she wrote in one of her letters. *There's no real chance of a tomorrow for us if you don't.* The worst thing about it was that he had never had these arguments with anyone else who had ever guessed what he did. ('It's better than that bomb,' one person had said to him. 'Anything's an improvement on Hiroshima and Nagasaki. If it stops the likes of that...') Some people would mention that Hitler had possessed thousands of tons of mustard gas in the last war. ('Do you think that maniac *wouldn't* have used it – if he'd thought we didn't have the same stored away in Sutton Oak? He wouldn't have hesitated. It saved all our lives, your hard work there.') They would shake their heads when they thought of this, pondering the likelihood of Armageddon.

In contrast to those people, Lillian seemed completely unshifting, never yielding an inch as a result of his arguments, never surrendering her point of view for the sake of peace between them.

'Oh God,' he kept saying to himself after yet another of their quarrels. 'Is there no hope?'

Occasionally, she would smile, giving him the same look she used to in the Talbot Inn. 'For goodness sake, John, it's not you I'm against. It's just the nature of your job. Why don't you accept that?'

But he couldn't. For this reason, he sometimes felt his temper surge within him. He wanted to smash something with his fist when the thought rose within him. He wanted to kick and lash out even against the steel of the boat, the weight of the rain that often whirled around him in the Minch. With one lunge of his hand, he could smash through the walls of this dining room, bring down all these Sutherland hills he did not know quite how to pronounce.

Stac Pollaidh, Suilven, Quinag, Cul Mor, Cul Beag…

His work was an integral part of him. Unlike Lambert who sat beside him at the table, for whom it was mainly a job, he believed in what he was doing – most of the time – here on the *Ben Lomond*. They had to protect themselves. As Shepherd had declared, they didn't want to leave themselves exposed as they had done in the early days of Hitler and the Nazis, when it was becoming clear that they might have to fight yet lacked the weapons to perform the task.

'None of us wants to fight another war. But if it happens, we've got to have the wherewithal to do it. Much though it might be distasteful to us to think of that.'

No. For all it was unpleasant at times, it was a necessary job to do. Time and time again, too, he reminded himself he wasn't alone in this belief, obtaining reminders of that fact every so often. Like the way other people praised the purpose of their work, even if they were unclear of its true nature. People such as the local dignitaries visiting the *Ben Lomond* tonight. John was introduced to them all, only to forget their names immediately. One was the Provost, another the Baillie, the third the Procurator Fiscal. The words meant nothing to him, never having heard of any of them before.

'Think of us as the Mayor, Deputy Mayor and the local judge,' the Provost told him. 'It might be easier that way.'

John nodded his head, smiling wryly as he pondered the chances of ever meeting people like that in his usual life in Salisbury or Liverpool. No chance. Far outside his orbit. He nodded his head and grinned when he was introduced to the others in the party: the bank manager, one of the town's lawyers, the President of the Rotary, the pipe band major, a pianist and a local singer. Together, they sat down to enjoy the meal the ship's chefs had prepared – roast potatoes, roast beef, Yorkshire pudding.

'Eat plenty,' Shepherd declared. 'This is one night of the year when rationing of any kind no longer applies.'

The same was true of the wine. Sitting in the company of Lambert and Parker, John found himself drinking more than he should do, swilling down glass after glass. He did this partly to suppress Lambert's mutterings by his side, the constant comments as he glanced in the direction of the gentlemen and ladies who were their honoured guests.

'I wonder if they know what we're doing in these waters. Or how little fuss we make when one of the local boats comes too close. The difference between that and the other day with the *Carella*. There was quite a hubbub then!'

'But I can understand that,' Parker said. 'If one of the fishermen here gets it, they can control it. There's only a small population. Most of them spend their lives in the one place, rarely travelling anywhere else. If this kicks off in Fleetwood, the next day it could be in Blackpool with all the holiday-makers crammed in there. The next it might be in Manchester or Leeds or London.'

'It hasn't stopped them experimenting in the big cities before this.'

'No. That's true. And they'll do it again.'

John's hand tightened on the glass. An image of Lillian came into his head, looking different than usual. She was sitting up in bed, her nightie sticking to her skin. Beads of sweat trickled down between her breasts. Her hair was tangled. She whimpered quietly from time to time.

'Have mercy… Lord, have mercy.'

He knew, even without touching it, that her forehead was hot and sweaty, clammy to the touch. He could smell the pain she was feeling, the aroma of death approaching, sneaking up on her bedside. He could sense, too, the fever she was suffering, and see the darkness about her face. Her cheeks and her eyes had been hollowed out by the plague, the power of the pestilence that had overwhelmed her.

'You brought me this,' she muttered. 'This was your gift to me.'

He tried to deny it, blaming the dark-haired stranger he had seen her with in his imagination, cursing him for being the carrier of the illness. He was the one who had brought it to her with his kisses, his embrace.

'No,' he muttered. 'It's not my fault.'

'Yes. It is,' she insisted, even in her illness, the labour of her breath. 'You're the one who treated animals in that way. You're the one who broke the covenant with the beasts.'

He could not deny her accusation, not even as he sat and tried to listen to the Provost's speech. The words reverberated in his head, spinning like the smoke that swirled around the space in which they were dining, the wine settling into the glasses into which it had been poured. Hell seemed to him a circular place, one in which long forgotten words keep revolving, the memories of past actions, half-forgotten deceptions and deceits continually come back around. He braced himself to try and hold onto his senses, all too aware that they were shifting loose from his fingers, escaping from his hold. Again, he focused on the Provost, trying to concentrate on the content of his speech.

'You're very lucky in where you're anchored,' the man was saying. 'The people of Lewis are extremely fortunate in the beauty of their island. They have wonderful archaeological monuments like the Callanish stones and the Carloway broch on the west side. They have no end of beautiful sandy beaches. Two of these are not far from where we are presently situated. There's the Tràigh Mhòr. No doubt you've seen the way it spreads out long and golden in the rare mornings when the sun shines. And then there's my own favourite, Garry. It is not only a beautiful beach – it even has caves. I used to hide in one when I was a child. There's also a marvellous stone bridge nearby that Lord Leverhulme, the soap king, built around a quarter of a century ago. Go and see it. Take the opportunity while you're here. But be warned. The road peters out at that point. It's known to everyone around these parts as the bridge to nowhere.'

Some of those on board laughed at this. John smiled faintly. It sounded too much like the road he was travelling these days.

'But don't forget about another aspect of island life. It has its sociable side, too. Next Friday, for instance, the Highland League side Inverness Caledonian is paying the island a visit. While they're here, they're playing against our Lewis Select team. Now, believe it or not, they're not a bad wee side. They enjoy their football here. One of the boys has even played for an English football side.'

'Which one?' someone guffawed. 'Shrewsbury?'

'I'll let you find that out for yourselves,' the Provost smiled. 'It'll help keep your interest and give you something to spot when you're there. Anyway, next Friday we'll not only have a football match but also a dance in the Town Hall afterwards. You're all very much welcome to attend – if, of course, your commanding officer gives you permission.'

He glanced towards Shepherd as he said this. A moment later and he was rewarded with the man's smile and nod. 'Of course,' Shepherd said. 'Though clearly we'll have to get these things organised beforehand.'

'Thank you, Mr Shepherd. Now, for those of you who don't gain the opportunity to spend time on our island, we thought we might give a taste – or a *blas* – of Scottish Gaelic, the language most commonly spoken here. Let me introduce you to a couple of young men who are going to entertain you with some Gaelic songs. One of them is a celebrated pianist who has played his music in a large variety of locations not just throughout these islands, but all across Europe. The other is someone who in recent years won the gold medal at our country's Gaelic music festival. Ladies and gentlemen, I give you welcome to the Hebrides…'

John missed the last few words and the names of the musicians. He looked up to see two young men making their way out of their seats to the piano where Wilson often sat, practising his music in the hours when he wasn't working in the laboratory. One, the pianist, was a strong, thickset individual, pushing up his sleeves as he sat down, giving a slight look of disapproval at the quality of the instrument he had before him. The other was both paler and thinner than his companion, with hollow cheeks, fair hair, a crisply pressed dark jacket. He was clearly the singer. Their opening number was slow, melancholic with the lilt and rhythm of the ocean. It washed over John as he sat there thinking of Lillian, how she was slipping through his fingers at present, like salt water, like the spill of sand upon the beach he could see nearby. He tried his best to hold onto her, but she was as elusive as both the melody and the tongue in which it was sung, all the time escaping and evading him as if she were being carried away like the sway of the tide.

It was the second song that he remembered afterwards. An example of what the young singer called 'mouth music', it was both stirring and rhythmic, shifting feet, forcing even the most glum and taciturn among the company to smile. The sounds that flowed from the singer's lips remained imprinted on John's consciousness even years later.

'Ic iarla nam bratach bàna
'Ic iarla nam bratach bàna
'Ic iarla nam bratach bàna
Chunna' mi do long air sàile

Hi 'illean beag ho ill o ro
Hi 'illean beag ho ill o ro
Hi 'illean beag ho ill o ro
Hu hoireann o hu o eileadh

Chunna mi do long air sàile
Chunna mi do long air sàile
Chunna mi do long air sàile
Bha stiùir òir oirr' 's dà chrann airgid...

Everyone applauded when the last notes died away. One or two cheered.

'What was that song about?' someone asked.

The singer blushed, slipping his hand into the inside pocket of his jacket.

'Oh, I thought someone might ask me that. It's a waulking song, one sung and composed by women when they worked the tweed. It goes way, way back. It's one I chose, too, because I was coming out here to sing on a boat at sea. The chorus is just complete nonsense, full of made-up sounds, but the song is about this longship with a helm of gold, two silver masts, rich red silk from Spain and white flags or banners trailing from it.

I'll read it to you.'

'The son of the earl of the white banners
The son of the earl of the white banners
The son of the earl of the white banners
I saw your longship on the sea

Hi 'illean beag ho ill o ro
Hi 'illean beag ho ill o ro
Hi 'illean beag ho ill o ro
Hu hoireann o hu o eileadh

I saw your longship on the sea
I saw your longship on the sea
I saw your longship on the sea
A helm of gold upon her and two silver masts...'

John didn't know whether the choice of words was accidental or deliberate. All he was conscious of in his imagination was that he could see the trail of vapour rising from the pontoon, concealing the coastline of the island in its thick, white sweep.

20

There were days when Jessie imagined some alternative existence for herself.

She'd picture herself on one of these great liners – the *Metagama, Canada* or *Marloch* – leaving Stornoway for Canada in 1923 or 1924, seeing her fellow islesmen and women thronging Number One Pier as they departed, hearing the words of the man from the Canadian Pacific company echoing across the deck. She'd contemplate being in one of the ports at which those vessels arrived – Saint John, Quebec, Montreal – and queuing up at customs, being questioned by immigration on arrival.

'Where is your birth certificate?'

'What is your intended occupation?'

'Do you have any relatives that have arrived here before you?'

She would have nodded her head in response to that one, aware that she had an uncle and aunt who had settled in Toronto, having arrived here sometime near the end of the nineteenth century. The *Metagama* had not been the first boat to leave this island. Many had sailed before it.

She'd picture, too, being in some of the places where she knew that people from her native village had settled, the ones written about in the scribbled notes of exiles or pictured in the postcards they sent home. They'd gain substance in her mind.

The bright and colourful plants of Vancouver. Holly, laurel, wisteria, rhododendron. All these shades and shapes she could only imagine from reading about in letters and newspapers, existing in their bright and vivid reality across the ocean. Forest, too. Dark and shadowy leaves and branches, tall tree trunks stretching miles into the unimaginable distance. Moss clinging to boughs. A nest hidden among green, visited by the occasional bird, a squirrel or some other animal scrambling among the twists and turns of wood. Foliage turning brown, purple, golden. Water, too. Not the shallow waters of Loch Bacabhat Chrois, with its row of crumbling shielings. Not Loch Mor na Gile, nor Loch na Cloich. Not even Loch Langabhat, for all that it is considered wide and long within these parts. Not the salt depths of the Atlantic or the Minch either, but instead the lakes existing on the far side of the ocean, bordered by mountains of immense and miraculous height, canyons and gorges hewed deep into rock, prairies with a flat emptiness that rolls out endlessly, much more even than the moor between Tolsta and Ness. No Muirneag. No Beinn Dail. No cliffs that sweep downwards when you reach land's sheer, sharp edge. No ridge or dip. Not a thin sliver of peat and sand, tapering out as her homeplace does at the island's various tips and edges, the Butt of Lewis, the peninsula of Point, the places where she had never been, where Lewis blurs into the slopes and peaks of Harris, where the hills of Uig fall and disappear into the sea.

And then there are the different buildings. Streets where one person's space encroaches into another, walls dividing one house from the next. Ornamented blocks of stores. Town halls. Hotels. Schools. Parks with drinking fountains, flower-filled gardens. Townships built of wood. Modern, temporary, inflammable, sometimes as damp and battered as her own. Painted window-sills – not just a grubby shade of white like all the houses possessed on the island, but red, yellow, brown. Wisps of smoke rising from fires fuelled by broken pieces of timber, leaves, tight coils of ivy, the broken branches of trees. Gravel roads. No pavements. And she'd picture herself walking along them, George or even Neil by her side, travelling southwards from Eastern Townships, Quebec, like so many of their counterparts after a short time there, slipping over the border to Vermont and beyond, going to Montpelier, Burlington, even across to New Hampshire as Neil sometimes did, mentioning those places in his letters home. The Winooski River. The Vermont State House. The portrait of George Washington on its wall. The stone bust of Abraham Lincoln. Neil had sent her pictures of some of these places and sights stuffed within an envelope.

Just to give you an idea of what things look like... he noted.

Sometimes she wondered what his wife might think of this, these epistles home, these pictures of his life there. Jessie remembered that, long before he left the island, she would catch him looking at her, his brown eyes following her movement as he worked in one of his neighbour's peats or harvesting oats or turnips, helping out on their croft. A swarthy, dark individual, she even recalled his gaze upon her as she said goodbye to George in Stornoway, the intensity of his look as she and Neil stood in the shade of Martin's Memorial Church that day. She had been aware of her attraction towards him then and was conscious of it throughout the years he had been married to another woman. Given the vast distance between the two of them, it had been a small, meaningless infidelity for her. However, she guessed it would have meant a little more to his wife.

Yet always somewhere in her visions of life on another continent, there was the thought of that return home, the one that Neil was now undertaking. She pictured him arriving at his home in Outer Coll, a place-name he had once joked about in one of his letters: *Jock said that whenever I tell anyone I come from Outer Coll in the Outer Hebrides, it makes me sound as though I hail from a distant planet in Outer Space. I laugh at him when he says that and tell him they only got one letter wrong when they named his village South Dell. They should have used the letter H instead of D.* For all he had been nearly thirty years away, there was still much that would be familiar. The gulls and oystercatchers. The hens scratching round the manure-heaps behind houses. The shit-smeared white and brown eggs. The barefoot, blue-eyed children running down to the Tràigh Mhòr or heading towards the school. The scrawny blackface sheep. The cattle. The women encased in black skirts and cardigans since the years of the First World War, if not before. All that had changed in them was that their hands and faces were more bruised, broken and worn with lifting up scythes in the absence of their men, bending their backs to harvest potatoes. And, of course, the heather, its tangle on the surface, twisting and turning more than the branches of any tree to be found in Vermont or Canada; brown, green, grey and purple, its roots deep within the peat that for centuries here had warmed them in the chill of winter; its ash, too, part of what enriched and fertilised poor soil, harvested from dead fires within their homes.

There would be changes also. The inevitable roll calls of death and birth. The alterations and improvements in houses. Thatch giving way to felt and tar. Stone knocked down and replaced by cement. The bus that Duncan drove, trundling through the village. The occasional tractor – grey and noisy, disturbing the peace – instead of the horse. The way in which there were more turnips grown, stored below turf beside byres that no longer stood alongside the family home. The talk, too, of the coming of electricity in the future. The prospect of an end to these visits to the wells found around the village, the women weighed down by aluminium pails, brimming over with fresh water.

And then there were those changes that she had barely registered, creeping up on her. It was those she looked forward to discovering when she wandered round the village with Neil, wandering across the machair round Tràigh Mhòr, seeing the glint of sand, the old dykes and lazybeds that had lain there for hundreds of centuries, signs of how they were tilled for centuries. There would be the yellow of buttercups and birds foot-trefoil, the red and blue of self-heal, ragged robin, northern marsh orchid. Purple autumn gentians spiking upwards from hollows scooped out near the beach. And all the small slopes and dips that made up the village crofts – Cnoc an Tairbh, Cnoc Glas, Cnoc an Eisg, Cnoc na Buaile – unknown to strangers but fixed in the minds of those who stayed here. She longed to take Neil round if that was what he chose to do, after they met in Stornoway, to familiarise him with the landscape to which he had returned, to echo the verses that were so often in her mind these days:

O's làidir na bannan gam tharraing a-null
Gu eilean beag donn MhicLeòid,
'S gu stiùir mi h-ealamh gu cala mo long
Nuair ruigeas mi ceann mo lò;
'S ma ghreimichas m' acair ri Carraig nan Al
Bidh m' anam tighinn sàbhailt beò,
Mo shiùil air am pasgadh am fasgadh Chill' Sgair
Le m' aithair 's mo mhàthair chòir.

O strong are the ties that are pulling me now
To the isle where MacLeod holds sway,
Guiding me to that port where I'll harbour my boat
On reaching the end of my days;
If my anchor holds on the Rock of Ages
My soul will come safely once more to life
When my sail is folded in Cill-sgair's shelter
Where with my father and mother I'll lie.

21

Roddy George was pontificating in a corner of the Lido, as was his wont to do.

'You know what I think lies behind this whole Revival nonsense? People here are desperate to lift their spirits. They've been under the cosh for years. One moment it's the First World War. The next it's the *Iolaire*, *Metagama*, the fishing industry crashing, World War Two. They haven't had relief or happiness in years. And so these people with their dog-collars and their Bibles have come along, offering hope and promise. Heaven after a grim time on Earth. So ordinary folk reach out and grab it. Anything to escape. Any corner. Any light in a darkened world.'

As he spoke, he brandished his hands, showing dust-stained fingers and broken nails from the work he was doing in the evening, building a byre behind his home. His features seemed to reflect his hard work, too: face chiselled by the wind, hair swept back from his forehead, eyes slate-grey. His words showed a similar intensity, a commitment to ideas. Sometimes, he pounded the table as he spoke, emphasising the importance of what he was saying. Along with the group of dockers who often visited the café during their work-breaks, there were a couple of East Coast fishermen in the far corner who would give him a baleful look every time he did this, mumbling between themselves. Duncan vaguely overheard what they were talking about – the word 'monkey' being spoken time after time, as if they were referring to the antics of his friend. On one occasion, Duncan mouthed an apology in their direction, receiving a shake of the head and a grin in response.

'Nutcase,' one of them muttered. 'The man's a nutcase.'

Duncan's other companion, Iain, was different: mild mannered and quiet. Every time he expressed a view, he half-undermined it with a giggle, as if he were terrified he might give offence. His features matched his reticence – fair, pale, thin, face slightly pock-marked. He looked as if he wanted to retreat into the shadows of the room, to go back home to Carloway on the west side of the island.

'Och, I don't know if you're right. Sometimes it's only in desperation that people find out the truth, both of themselves and the world. Sometimes it's only in utter darkness that people can even catch a glimpse of light.'

'You sound as if you're tempted, Iain.'

He coughed before answering. 'So what if I am? It seems to me that in almost every case, faith offers a better model for living than any offered by people without it.'

'It also has more hypocrites, as anyone would know from looking round this place.'

'As our minister said to me, hypocrisy isn't the worst offence. At least the people who are guilty of it are trying to be good. That isn't the case with those who revel in being cruel or greedy. They're quite happy being that way.'

Duncan tuned out of the exchange, barely listening anymore. Unsure exactly where he stood, he was always troubled by this kind of conversation. Too many people had certainties where he only had questions. He had experienced a conversation with his own minister a short time before, and he had admitted he had doubts. 'Just trust in the Lord,' the minister had said. 'Remember, He can save you, even if you're halfway between the stirrup and the ground, the cliff-top and the wave...' Duncan had shaken his head, another host of questions crowding in, and turned away from the man.

He wondered, too, if it was the case that the people here on the island had experienced a more unfortunate last forty or so years than those from anywhere else. Was it even remotely true? He had wandered through London shortly after the end of the war, noting the buildings in ruins, the hopelessness in people's faces. Hadn't they suffered just as much? He was aware of how the ordinary people of Gibraltar had been sent elsewhere during the conflict – to Madeira, Ballymena, London – and were now trying to pick up the strands of their past existence in a place where they had been mistrusted and treated with suspicion by the same authorities who were now overseeing them again. Hadn't they experienced grief and loss, too? And then there was the likes of Luigi, serving coffee and lemonade to the customers who crowded into the café where he worked, forced – like so many Hebrideans – to leave his native country in search of work. He had spent much of his years of war in the Isle of Man, a prisoner on another island. One time he had talked to Duncan about the *Arandora Star*, the ship carrying Italian and German prisoners to Canada that had been sunk somewhere between Northern Ireland and the Hebrides in 1940.

'Many of the dead were washed up in Colonsay. I always think of that and compare it to the *Iolaire*. In some ways, both my peoples ended up in places like that.'

Roddy George nudged Duncan, conscious that his friend was trapped in his own thoughts – as he often was lately.

'You got any news?' he asked.

'No. Not really,' Duncan replied.

'What about the football team? You heard who's playing on the Select side?'

'A couple of lads from the Back team. Rodo, Mac Ullag from Coll. Alex Macleod. The other one is Dan Macaskill. Sheorais a Bhideanaich's son, from Lighthill. Anyone else you know?'

'A few. Angus Martin – from Lochs – who plays for United. They call him Bobby. Bill Cameron from the School. He used to play for some Highland League team a few years ago. Stoodie and Hoddan from Point.'

'Both fine players. Stoodie turned out for Mansfield a few years ago. A great talent. Hoddan's a fine Gaelic singer. One of the best of the young ones.'.

'And then there's Alex Macdonald, "Marco" from Carloway,' Iain interjected. 'Larry Maciver, too. You're forgetting to recognise real quality.'

'Oh, no show without Punch,' Roddy George grinned. 'You have to mention two of your own.'

'Larry's playing at outside left. If it had been up to you to mention him, he'd have been left outside.' Iain winked.

'Don't I know it,' Roddy George said, prodding his friend with a playful punch. 'The only two from Carloway in the team. They're going to have their work cut out, you know. Inverness Caley have a good side. Terrific in attack. There's Andy "Jupie" Mitchell, a great goal-scorer. The same is true of Donnie "Ginger" Mackenzie. He had a trial for Newcastle. And then there's Donnie Mackintosh. He played for Rangers for a while. Really fast on his feet. Some wonderful players.'

'Our boys are good, too.'

'Aye. But they're going to have a real challenge against this crowd. It'll be a good game.'

'Aye...'

It was at that moment Duncan's mouth went dry. Ina had just stepped in with Janet, one of her friends from the tweed mill, and they were standing at the counter, waiting for Luigi to serve them. He took her all in. Her straight fair hair framed by a picture on the wall of some Italian square with a fountain jetting water straight upwards (a different direction to the way it would be experienced in Stornoway: blowing into your face). A faint flush was on her cheeks, nerves causing her to tremble. He was conscious, too, that she was breathing hard, the slow movement of her breasts, her legs below her tweed coat. When she was served, she turned around, bringing her coffee to a nearby table with Janet leading the way. As she did so, she looked up for a moment, smiling in his direction.

'Hello,' she said.

He nodded in return, barely able to speak, Rockitis taking his words away. 'Hello, Ina.'

'We were wondering why you weren't spending so much time in the library these days,' Roddy George whispered. 'Clearly something caught your attention outside its walls.'

Part Three

Sèist

– chorus

Mi Le M'Uilinn

Sèid sèimh socair o ghaoth tuath
Gus an cuir i Cluaidh as fàir

My Elbow on my Knee

North wind, blow gentle and blow kind
Until the Clyde is far behind.

By Murdo Macfarlane – Murchadh MacPhàrlain

22

After reading it several times, John crumpled the letter he had received from Lillian in his fingers. Despite this, every word remained with him, searing his thoughts, colliding with everything he did all day.

My darling John,

I hope you're well in whatever far, forsaken part of the world you happen to be in at the moment. No doubt I'll be able to guess where you've been by the tone and shade of your skin. If you've a tan, I'll suppose you were in the Bahamas or Bermuda. If you look pale and grey, I'll just think that you've been somewhere dull and dismal, like the north of Scotland or Iceland, away from the rest of us and contact with the sun.

Anyway, there's no doubt we'll have a lot to sort out when we meet again. There's the way you distrust and dislike me every time you imagine I look at another man. Sometimes your jealousy is just ridiculous. You are even suspicious and unsure of me every time I speak to Billy the Lip. Do you have any idea how crazy that is? What's wrong with you when you behave that way? And then there's the way you go on about my people's faith, as if you think I'm going to betray you in that too: wake up one morning and become a born-again Christian. You really do try to have it all ways. One minute, you think I'm going to run away with some man in a bar. The next, you seem to believe that I'm going to be shouting hallelujah all the time. It says a lot more about you than me that you can keep both these things in your head at the same time.

Yet there is more than that we have to talk about. I really can't stand the job you do. Men and women can be judged on the way they treat children and animals, how they handle the weak and defenceless. So what are you doing? Killing frogs, monkeys, mice? And for what reason? None that make any sense to me. But for all that, I still want you in my life. For all that I don't like your job. Or your mother dripping poison into your ear because she's the one who made a couple of stupid mistakes in her life. No. I want you remaining by me all the time and not going off to unknown, secret places where it's impossible to reach you. I want you in a job that I can tell my relatives and friends about and boast about in the world. I want someone I can trust and can also trust me...

He was unable to escape her, always in his thoughts, even as he stood there washing the array of beakers, funnels, flasks, Petri dishes and measuring cylinders they had been using in the laboratory, ensuring each one was clean, dipping them into soap suds to wash out every last drop of whatever concoction had been contained within them. There were times he wished he could do that to himself, find some sort of cleansing agent that could wash out every last drop of suspicion, every stain and smear of doubt, even the recollections he had of the soft sweetness of her body as she lay naked beside him in their bed.

'You've done this before,' he had muttered on their first night together.

'No,' she said. 'A little heavy petting perhaps, but never more than that. My mother's lectures always held me back. I could always hear her speaking to me.'

'But you were so enthusiastic.'

'That's because I'm just like most young women. Pretty desperate to try.'

'Oh… I promise to give you ample opportunity.'

She laughed as they embraced again, feeling her breasts against his chest, her legs locking his.

He needed to find some means to remove her from his head – and one that would make all thought of the *Carella* disappear. Chase away the prospect of the vessel arriving in Fleetwood, its crew passing on the plague to the people of that port, the members of Lillian's family crowding the pews of their church, passing on death with a clasp of hands, a pat on the back of a friend or neighbour.

'How you doing? Good to see you again.' And then, a day or two later, the warmth of that welcome passing on the chill of death to the person that had been touched.

Perhaps they would have been better sinking the *Carella*, removing that trawler from the waves with a bomb or a torpedo, sinking it somewhere off the coast of Islay or Jura, pretending it had struck a rock or gone swirling down a whirlpool, been caught in the snare of another fishing boat's nets. At least then only its crew would have been lost. No possibility of thousands of men and women tumbling to their deaths around the edge of Morecambe Bay – with himself forever implicated in it, his job making him partly responsible for the loss of all their lives. No prospect of the plague travelling from town to town, city to city.

He hurried the thought from his head, conscious that – for this one night – he had the opportunity to forget about all of this. Tonight was when this football match was to be played. Lambert had reminded him of it, sidling up to him when he stood at the sink, his fingers caught and wrapped in a bubble of white froth, a glass jug in his grip.

'You going to the game?'

'No chance,' John grinned, lightening for once. 'I stayed for years in Liverpool and never once went to see Billy Liddell or Bert Stubbins. Don't think I'm going to bother going to see a bunch of hairy Highlanders running after a ball. They're not quite in the same league, are they?'

'No. I don't suppose they are. But I am going to clean myself up and go to Stornoway. Visit one of the pubs there. It's long enough since I had a pint or two.'

'Long enough since any of us had that.'

And with that mere mention of a pub, John once more found himself gazing at the image on the mirror advertising Burtonwood Top Hat, the beer he often watched Lillian pour from a gold tap behind the bar. The figure there, with his high-peaked headgear, his aristocratic choice of clothes, seemed to be grinning at him, the way he always did when he had taken a drink or two too many or when Lillian appeared to be paying too much attention to a customer.

He wondered what the pubs in a small town such as Stornoway would be like, picturing them as similar to the Talbot back in Liverpool, with its grubby public bar with bare boards, old men brooding over pints with their dogs stretched out alongside, playing dominoes on the tables before them, checking too the results of the horse races – if they had such things this far north.

And the likes of the saloon bar where she worked. Its large round clock on the wall, set five minutes too early in order that they might chase the customers out at nine. The labelled bottles of ales and spirits, all glistening and shining. Polished gold of beer taps. The murmured conversations of couples around the room.

23

It was Seonaid who spruced Jessie up for the occasion, bringing products to her home that she had only read about in a newspaper before. There was Palmolive soap, which – according to an advert she had seen – 'brings out beauty while it cleans your skin'. There was Bristow's Lanolin Cream Shampoo, which 'blesses your hair with sun-lit beauty.'

The younger woman cleaned out the dirt that had gathered below the rims of Jessie's nails, rinsed and lathered her curls, tugging a brush and comb through locks as she sat on her kitchen chair facing the window, the pages of the *Stornoway Gazette* spread out on the floor. Last week's headlines caught her attention from time to time: the number of fish brought to Stornoway harbour; the tale of a fight in a country hall recorded in the accounts of the Sheriff Court.

'It's been a while since you did this,' Seonaid said.

'Probably a few years,' she confessed. 'I was hoping to leave this job to the undertaker. At least he would get paid for it.'

Seonaid laughed. 'I must admit that the only time I ever make a fuss of myself is in the week before Murdo comes home. That's when these things come out of storage.' She fished a bottle out of her shopping bag, setting it on the kitchen table. 'Here's something else I brought for you. You can give yourself a spray of it before you go out.'

Jessie squinted at it. 'Yardley English Lavender. What is it?'

'What every woman needs sometimes. Perfume.'

'Oh… give over,' Jessie laughed, slapping out her hand at her companion. 'At my age? I'll need a lot more than that. Probably need to be sprayed with disinfectant to clean the mould off.'

'Och, you don't need that! You scrub up very well without it. Some women half your age don't look as good as you.'

'But what about the cracks? I need to find a way of covering them up.'

'I have that, too,' Seonaid grinned, pulling another item from your bag. 'Powder to make your skin grow pale. Cover up more than a few cracks. Not that you have many. Tone down some of your blushes.'

'Seonaid. Why would I blush? I'm not going out on a date.'

'Stop pretending! When were you last out in a man's company?'

'Oh, with Duncan the bus-driver, down at the shore a little while ago.'

'That doesn't count. When were you last out on a date?'

'It's not a date.'

'Come on. When was it?'

'A long time ago.'

'When?'

Jessie herself took a long time before answering. '21st April 1923.'

'When?'

She repeated the date, recalling the events of that time clearly. She could see George again, standing on the step to Martin's Memorial Church, feeling once more the touch of his lips on her skin. She remembered the smart tweed jacket he was wearing, kitted out for exile, glimpsing, too, Neil as he had been that day, his eyes watching them as they stood there. She recalled, too, the thought that the moment would soon come when her own life would be transformed, following George to his new home across the Atlantic. Time had cracked open that day, for all she never realised it back then. A gulf – larger than any that sometimes split cliffs near Tolsta, perhaps even than the one that separated the west coast of Lewis from the edge of America – appearing in her life. This was the first time she had ever made any attempt to bridge it, for all that she feared it might – like the structure that Leverhulme had built some thirty years ago on the far edge of the village – take her nowhere.

Seonaid stopped, too, aware of the effect that her words had on Jessie. 'It is a long time, nearly thirty years. But on the good side, take a look at yourself. For someone who is nearly fifty, you're fit and well. It must be all that walking and working hard you do. Good for people. Good for you. It makes you look a lot younger than you actually are.'

'I still feel the aches.'

'Oh, we all feel them from time to time. Even at my age.'

Jessie heard the clip of the scissors as Seonaid worked away at the back of her head. Unlike many of the woman in the village, she didn't tie her hair up in a tight bun. Her locks were much too thick and unruly for that. Instead, there was the occasional tidy-up from Mairead, perhaps, or Seonaid. Of the two of them, Seonaid was the more natural hairdresser, her fingers more nimble, her grip more firm and secure. There were times, though, when she missed Mairead, her chat more familiar, the years they had spent together in Tolsta more alike. The two of them had so much in common, friends for a long time, the occasional loneliness of a single life.

'It can't be easy for you,' Jessie said. 'Raising a son when Murdo's away most of the time.'

'It's probably easier here than most places,' Seonaid replied. 'It's almost normal here – so many away for months on the Hydro, in the Merchant Navy, or even at the whaling.'

'I suppose… It's what people have to do to raise a family in these parts, go away from the island. You can't get by on pennies.'

'Aye. Nor can you feed yourself all that well on scenery. As someone once said to me.'

'That's true.'

And then there was what the two women didn't mention: the nature of some of those who stayed at home. Jessie could see one of them from her kitchen window as Seonaid ran scissors through her hair – old Uilleam making his way through his croft to his home. His calloused fingers held a pitchfork before him as though he were counting out the steps, using the prongs to mark his trek. Waiting for him in his house was his wife, Mairi. She always complained that he spent most of his life like this, measuring out everything in a mean and grudging fashion, every penny that he spent. Jessie had heard Mairi describe the man as a miserly skinflint with even farthings jailed and imprisoned in his hand. Yet when he died, these words would be forgotten. He would be praised as frugal and thrifty, someone who was careful with his cash.

She had seen the same happen to a few other men on the island. The ones who were once viewed as brutes regarded as men of energy and passion when they passed away. Those who liked a drink became people who relished life, no matter how their habits affected others. It was sometimes war that did this, altering and transforming the dead in the memory of those who knew them. Sometimes it was absence, causing memory to shift and bring about changes that had not been in evidence before. Years spent far away. In the Merchant Navy. In Vermont. She had to be careful not to let perfume cloud her thoughts, give into that kind of thinking. Not tomorrow. Not the next day. Not any time after that.

24

Duncan found himself behaving in a way he normally never did when he started the bus that morning: checking the rear-view mirror; looking, too, at the side-view mirrors even before stepping onto the vehicle. He did this not for the usual reasons, aware there was little danger any vehicle was coming his way down a side-road to his home in Tolsta at that time of day, but to make sure he looked fine, that his chin was shaved as smoothly as possible, his hair neatly brushed and his shirt and trousers ironed and pressed. For once, these things mattered. He wanted to look his very best. Smart. Clean. Presentable. In the way he'd done when he mingled with military men in Gibraltar, visiting the garrison, going down to the Universal Café in Main Street where a crowd from the Docks Operating Group had gathered. One of them spent his time wanting to declare war on the Yanks when the conflict was over.

'Can't come soon enough. One of them stole my wife. You know that? One of them stole my bloody wife! You welcome these bastards to the country and they behave like that! Ungrateful, nasty crowd!'

Another had joined in the chorus, planning mutiny against their officers if a US warship came near the Straits.

'We'll take over the guns and blow them out of the water!'

Duncan hoped there would be no conversations like that tonight, for all that he was aware that the football crowd even here on the island were capable of being overcome by their own frenzies. He recalled one time the local Back team had been beaten 5–1 by a side from Point.

'Five lucky breaks! That's all it was! Five lucky breaks!' one shouted.

'Aye… And most of them called Stoodie,' someone else responded, referring to the nickname of one of the players from Point.

'Oh, shut up!'

Today would be long and difficult. He knew that. There would be a couple of extra journeys by its end. One to take the football supporters into town. After that, there would be the drive home, followed by a return to Stornoway to take a few to the late-night dance. Then a turn around when the final notes of the accordion and guitar died away, the rhythm of the last waltz coming to an end. He would then return to Tolsta – to toss and turn within his bed for a few restless hours – before taking the bus back to town once more. His whole life on an endless loop till Sunday morning.

But it wasn't that occupying his thoughts. Instead, they kept spinning in the direction of Ina, the woman whom more than any other person filled his mind these days. He had discovered a bit about her in the last while. She stayed in the village of Balallan, a long stretch of houses in Lochs at the south end of the island, not that far from the boundary with Harris with all its high, heather-crowned hills. She worked in James Mackenzie's tweed mill, brushing the finished cloth, snipping away the occasional twist or turn of thread that had come loose. 'She'll make a great crofter's wife,' Roddy George had teased him. 'Good in the peats and the fields. Plenty of Gaelic.'

Secretly pleased, Duncan smiled when Roddy George said this. Sometimes, girls from the town found it difficult to settle in the villages. They lacked the necessary skills with the peat-blade. Often they didn't have a word of Gaelic despite being surrounded by those who spoke the tongue their whole lives.

He turned the ignition, listening to the slow thrum of the engine before setting off. The first passenger he picked up was Uisdean, a few years older than him. A bonnet pressed on his bald head, he was one of the elders in the Free Presbyterian Church in the village, occasionally stepping on the bus for a meeting elsewhere. He would frown as he spoke about how he had been on HMS *Hood* in 1940 when the Royal Navy had attacked the French fleet at Mers-el-Kébir in French Algiers.

'We were lucky. God was looking after us,' he would say every time he raised the subject. 'We came out of that one safe and well. The ship was in quite a mess. Not really fit to sail. One of the worst boats in the Navy.'

Duncan said nothing, aware that because of that day the people of Gibraltar had come to fear the French almost as much any other nation in the war. 'They bombed a convent school there a wee while afterwards,' he had once remarked to Uisdean. 'At least, most thought it was them.'

'Were there any priests or nuns wounded or killed?'

'A couple of nuns wounded.'

'You don't expect me to mourn them,' Uisdean muttered. 'One bunch of Catholics killing another.'

Duncan recalled there were times when he'd even stepped into the Catholic cathedral there, looking at the pictures of the Virgin Mary on the wall, the crucifix like the cross-trees of the sailing ships he had sometimes seen travelling down the

Minch in his youth. It had all been strange and alien to him, a multitude of shades and colours compared to the simple brown and white of the churches at home. He remembered standing a short distance away from the Polish leader, Sikorski, lying in state there after his plane had gone down into the sea nearby, killed, perhaps, by the Russians who saw him as a threat to their rule. Mumbling the Lord's Prayer to himself, he had pretended to make the sign of the Cross, fumbling as he did so. He didn't imagine he convinced anyone around when he did this, least of all the Poles who were weeping at the loss of their great man. He felt just as alien on those rare occasions when he stepped into the King's Chapel near the Governor's Residence – its flags and stained glass at odds, too, with the plainness of the church he knew from home.

Yet he had never disliked the differences between faiths and places. Just noted that they belonged to a landscape a line of latitude or two away from his own. In this, he was very different from Uisdean. Or from his own father; for all that he rarely spoke, he occasionally muttered his opinion of both Catholics and the East Coast fishermen, whom they occasionally glimpsed fishing in the waters nearby.

'Robbers and thieves. Robbers and thieves.'

Once, he even added another couple of words to his list of condemnations.

'Pirates and murderers.'

When Duncan asked him why he felt this way, he snorted, adding a few extra syllables to his denunciation.

'1862. Buckie boat ramming the *Christina*. Didn't even throw the drowning men from Ness a rope.'

After that, there was not another word from him. Just the

sense of him brooding on an ancient wrong. Duncan was aware, though, that both Uisdean and his father were not alone in thinking like that; he was conscious that there was a distrust of Catholics among his companions. He had heard Roddy George and one or two of the dockers become steamed up about it, how they were 'idolators' and 'blasphemers'. Occasionally it was the East Coast fishermen who sat in the Lido Café or one of the town's bars that stirred up enmity and dislike.

'Stealing our fish. We can barely make a living in these parts.'

What made people think and talk like that? What caused them to be that way?

He washed away the thought from his mind, stopping the bus to allow on two young men. They were a little like him – smart, spruced up, neat. Clearly they would be going to the football match that evening. What he didn't expect, however, was the passenger he picked up at the final stop in the village.

Jessie.

Looking years younger than she had been for a decade or two.

Jessie.

With the aroma of perfume wafting all around her.

25

Gulls followed the motorboat as the men left the *Ben Lomond* behind on their way to Stornoway for their one night ashore in a hotel there. The birds' screeching, squawking cries formed an undercurrent to the noise of the engine, their grey and white feathers coming together to form small storm-clouds in the sky. Once or twice they even streaked the motorboat and a few of those onboard with excrement, falling like drops of rain. Life shifted back to its basics, sea-spray soaking the men's faces as the vessel on which they had spent so much time over the last few months shrank into the distance.

'I wonder what's the collective word for them,' Lambert mused. 'A plague of gulls. A pestilence. That's what they should call them anyway, with all their shite and racket.'

'Not to mention how they feast upon the dead,' John said, recalling how he had seen a group of them feeding on a sheep on the edge of the shoreline a few days before, the sweep of his binoculars capturing the movement of wings.

'They've pretty nasty habits.'

Wilson pushed back the throttle of the small boat. It gathered speed, the peninsula ahead coming into closer view. They lurched from side to side until their balance was restored.

'You think these birds know what we're up to here?'

'Oh, I doubt it,' John smiled. 'They're just the usual seagull cries. Not distress calls.'

'They might think we're a fishing boat. Like the one they're keeping an eye on.'

'The *Carella*?'

'Yes. The one from Fleetwood.'

'They're going to be disappointed if they do. Not much herring here. Not so much as a sprat.'

As John said this, the image of the boat crashed into his mind again, how it had made it through the Minch that day, its crew deaf to all the clamour that was going on around them. Another thought came to him. He wondered if they had distributed the fish caught by the vessel, selling them in the market on the pier, sending them out to the merchants and chippies all around the north-west of England, serving them in kitchens and restaurants, the occasional bar or hotel. Perhaps the government hadn't thought of this – the possibility of the plague being passed on by droplets of mist clinging to the silver skin of cod, seeping into its white flesh. He shivered at the thought of it, that poison being passed on by the exchange of notes and coins, the small change given by mothers to their children to spend at the local fish shop.

And always at the centre of these thoughts, Lillian, sitting at a table with her parents, raising a fork to her mouth.

'It's a disgrace we're here,' Lambert muttered.

'What do you mean?'

'In this place. At the country's edge. And the whole place looks so peaceful. All these fields. Moors. Tiny houses. Beaches. So calm and innocent. Almost like a children's toy town. And now we're bringing war to its shores. A part of the world that looks as if it's been untouched by it.'

'I doubt that's true. Mackay was talking about that the other night, how when he was in the Navy during the war, they visited some loch in the Highlands a few times. Loch Horrible they called it. It was where the U-boats surrendered at the end of the war.'

'Oh, I didn't know that. But you're probably right. After all, according to what we've been told, the place has lots of churches in it. Always a sign.'

'What do you mean?'

'They're always good for war. *They said this mystery never shall cease: The priest promotes war, and the soldier peace.'*

'And who came out with that one?'

'Blake again. The one my wife is always quoting at me.'

'Oh. I hadn't heard that one before.' He sighed, looking towards the sea once again. There were a couple of boats heading towards port. He took note of the letters written on their side – *SY360*, *PD272*, *FR196*, *CY26*, names like *Larkspur* and *Silver Crescent* – and wondered if they were heading to Stornoway for the football match, the late-night dance or the pub. Probably a mixture of all three. 'It's probably experienced war in different ways from us. Loads of women made widows. Men killed or injured. Children without fathers. But there's never been a bomb dropped on it. No one killed that way.'

'You're probably right,' Lambert said. 'And now we're here with our monkeys and guinea pigs. Gases and sprays. Carrying out tests near its shores. A thousand new ways of killing a man. And we're bringing all of that to them. Not that they know anything about it.'

'I wouldn't bet on that,' John said grimly. 'It's a small community. And nothing goes faster round a small community than gossip. And you can bet your bottom dollar that we're the ones being gossiped about.'

* * *

A thousand nudges let Jessie know she was the one being talked about on the bus that morning. Winks being passed from neighbour to neighbour. Fingers pressed against lips. A chorus of whispers behind her. She knew from years of experience what they were saying.

'*Seall oirre se.*'

'*Càil i dol?*'

'*De seòrsa fàileadh a' th'oirre?*'

She was conscious even when they reached the school, the questions would continue, the women's attention drawn as they had been that day when she stood below the spire with George. Back then there would have been glances, raised eyebrows, looks of horror if they had noticed a hurried, furtive kiss. This time there would be gazes following the direction in which she travelled, noting each turn and twist she took upon her journey. There would be some who even passed on word to their neighbours, those they knew in Stornoway, asking them to keep an eye out for the stranger in their midst, the one with neatly cut hair, a smart tweed coat and black polished shoes, the reek of perfume trailing from her wherever she goes.

'It should be easy enough to sniff her from a distance. She seems to have taken a bath in the stuff.'

And then there was the one who dared to ask her – Morag Morrison, from Gress, leaning forward from her seat, directing the question towards her in a loud voice.

'So where are you off to today, Jessie?'

She took a moment before answering, conscious that every voice in the bus had stilled to hear her reply.

'I've an appointment,' she declared.

'Oh, where?' Morag's friend Catriona responded. 'At the hospital?'

She decided to nod, relieved she didn't have to speak or tell a lie.

'Oh, what's the problem?' Catriona spoke this time. It was as if their voices were interchangeable, slipping from one mouth to another.

'A check-up,' Jessie replied, wondering if she might go further, announce to one and all that she had 'some problems with her heart', but that would probably be a mistake. It would only make her fellow passengers wonder about her heart problem, and how perfume, powder and a new hairstyle might possibly cure it. Instead, she bit her lip, hoping this would be enough for those who quizzed her, knowing if they asked any more they would be intruding into her privacy, becoming those who were talked about themselves.

'Oh…' Catriona said.

'Hope it all goes well for you,' Morag added.

'Thank you very much,' she smiled, thinking of the route she would have to take now that these questions had been asked. Instead of going directly to the café where she'd agreed to meet Neil, she would have to go up Church Street, pretending to head in the direction of the hospital before doubling back on her steps and slinking off to meet him.

Life could become very complicated on a small island.

It might be easier elsewhere.

* * *

Duncan shifted gears of the bus as he journeyed through Tong, taking the long curve at the edge of village. He couldn't help wondering how that discovery on Tràigh Mhòr had affected both him and Jessie that day. Today, the two of them were on the bus kitted out in their smartest, wearing their neatest, most well-pressed clothes. They had both been altered and transformed since that moment, becoming less and like their normal selves.

What kind of spell had been cast on them?

Would life ever return to normal again?

26

Right from the moment John stepped on the quay, it was an alien landscape to him. Smelling of fish and seaweed. The reek of smoke from some of the small boats. The musty dampness of sea and rain. Oil spillage. Around the harbour, fishing nets coiled and curled, draped on the pier, hung out to dry on lines. He could see the glint of hooks among some of them, bare bright steel within the darkened web. A cluster of creels, too, stacked beside a bollard. A rope tied and knotted round it, straining to hold a vessel. A castle across the bay. Stone wall. A red-doored building. Keys dangling from the ignitions of vans and cars. Some with doors left open. Others with windows rolled down.

'You wouldn't do that in our place,' Lambert laughed.

'Not for two seconds.'

'That's at least something to be said for the pious Scottish bastards who live round here.'

John could hear, too, lorries, their noise as strange and foreign to them as the steadiness of land. The beep of a horn as someone passed a friend. The roll of a barrel – full or empty – across the pier. Voices speaking Gaelic, words indecipherable as seagull cries echoed round the harbour. The whistling of an unknown song. Men shouting out in a variety of English that was equally hard to distinguish.

He looked across at Lambert. 'What the hell are they saying?'

Lambert shrugged. 'No point in asking me. I think they're Dutch.'

'Double-Dutch.'

'Gaggling-Gaelic.'

'Scrambled-Scotch.'

It was the same when they stepped into shops – with names like Nicolson, Maclean, Morrison and Smith emblazoned on the store fronts. It was about all that was going on they could understand. Step through a shop door and life quickly became even more of a mystery. He asked for a *Manchester Guardian* and received only a blank look in return.

'We've got the *Record* and the *Express*,' the assistant said. '*The People's Journal*?'

He shook his head, barely able to respond. 'No. No thanks,' he said, never having heard of two of the papers.

And then there were the clothes people wore. The cloth caps squeezed down on heads. The occasional man in dungarees. An array of tweed jackets. Thick, warm jerseys. A white-collared, black-suited minister or two, wearing a Homburg hat and clutching a copy of the *Daily Express* as they went on their way. Sometimes, they would stop and talk to those who were clearly their parishioners, asking questions about their welfare. 'How are you feeling today, Murdo?' There were a few school pupils, too, striding down the street with the confidence and gusto of the young.

What most astonished him was the number of women dressed in black. Mourning-coloured scarves wrapped around heads. Grief-tinted coats and skirts. Sorrow-darkened cardigans. It seemed to him that even on a calm sunlit day like today, there was much woe and gloom clouding Stornoway's streets and pavements, a catalogue of clothes recording loss and bereavement, the passing of those who they were once close to in life. He wound his way through it all, noting an older woman in a tweed coat, her grey hair neatly groomed as she accompanied a man who was clearly American down the town's main street. His light clothes and tartan shirt provided a sharp contrast in shade from the rest of the people, and his presence was clearly drawing their attention.

'God. It's a gloomy place,' he muttered to Lambert. 'A bridge to nowhere. Just like that mayor of theirs was talking about.'

'It is that,' Lambert replied. 'Perhaps we should go to one of the churches. It might cheer us up.'

'I doubt that,' he laughed. 'Think we should go the pub instead.'

'There's a few in the town. As many as there are churches. Saw that as we were passing. When they open, we'll head there.'

'Good idea.'

It was at that moment they saw a group of young women walking along the main street, turning to go into one of the two Italian cafés they had noticed in the town.

'Think we should follow them,' Lambert grinned. 'I haven't seen one of them in months.'

The impact of memory made John reel once more. Lillian came back into his mind, aware that other men must look at her in the same way Lambert's eyes followed this group of young women, taking in her long dark hair, the easy rhythm of her step, her high heels, red lipstick. He was conscious, too, she might be in danger, that the white veil of gas that had clouded the *Carella* might bring its poison to the streets of the town where she lived.

* * *

Jessie had never walked among trees before. Always the shore or moorland. The squelch and slap of the latter. Its sludge and occasional slither. The brush of bracken. Rough twists and turns of heather. The sense of its depths and darkness below each movement of her feet. Always, too, the wind against her, making her hair and clothes flap, as if her every step met with resistance, an invisible force. It was different in the castle grounds. The wind was somehow gentler there, for all its work was still in evidence: an occasional tree trunk lying at a slant, a broken branch, shattered twigs. A bush jostling into a space once occupied by a willow, sycamore or spruce. Other things occurred to her – how the underside of a leaf seemed often to be a different shade from the other, how branches swished from side to side, trunks sometimes looked coarse and gnarled. There were also aspects that had escaped her attention before, how some of the bushes had bright and brilliant flowers, how others had cones. There was also the way she did not know the name of just about anything that grew there. Neil told her what the trees might be called as he walked along the track beside her.

'I can't be sure if I'm right,' he confessed. 'They're not the same as the ones I see in Vermont. Very different.'

'What kind are there?'

'Birch, beech, elm, ash, the white pine. And, of course, the sugar maple. They make golden maple syrup from that. I took a couple of bottles with me to give to people when I came home. A different kind of sweetness.' He paused for a moment, as if recalling the taste. 'And then there's the leaves on the trees.

How they change shades in the fall. That's what they call the autumn over there. Become gold, red, yellow, purple.'

'Like the heather here turning purple in August?'

'Aye. But more than that. As if the whole world around us has been dipped in paint.'

'You like it there?'

A crow cawed out from the upper branches, startling her as she walked along. It was a sound she rarely heard out on the moor. For all that they were sometimes to be found there, it was as if these birds took a vow of silence among its empty acres, leaving the curlew, snipe, gull or lapwing to call out instead.

'It took a long time to get used to it. I missed the sea. Even the way the salt within it used to thaw out any snow that ever fell on us rapidly and quickly. We were miles away from it there. A different kind of world all together. No doubt about that. The white pine used to remind me of how far we'd crossed. They used the tree to create masts for sailing ships. Every time I looked at one, I thought of that. Making a boat for myself and going home.'

She looked over at Neil. For all the greyness of his hair and the light colours of his American clothes, his mood had darkened since leaving these shores, a change reflected in the shade and thickness of his thick black eyebrows. Like thunderclouds dimming his intense brown eyes, they needed to be trimmed. She was aware of shadows within him that she had not been conscious of when he was younger. With his dislocation had come a sadness, a longing for what he had left behind.

'Did you think of that a lot?'

'Oh, all the time. When I'd be working in the shop, I'd catch myself singing a Gaelic song and think how nice it would be to hear that language around me all the time.'

'And what about your wife?'

'Oh, she didn't have Gaelic,' he laughed. 'Didn't even like it when Jock and I spoke in that tongue. Or the few others, too, I could talk with on the other side of Canadian border, the Eastern Townships in Quebec. Not that there's many remaining there these days. Most of them travelled south years ago. Settled somewhere or other in the States. Even as far to the west as Vancouver or Oregon. All over the place. I remember only too well how she used to react when I spoke in that tongue to anyone. "Oh, you're back among the heather again. Don't you think it's about time you scraped it off your boots?" No. She was from Ayrshire. If she talked about her home, it was always the Harbour and Rabbie Burns. Not that she could come out with a single line the man ever wrote. It was up to Jock Murray to do that.'

'You don't sound as if you found her easy to live with?'

He stopped, standing on the path for a moment or two. 'She wasn't easy, no. Especially towards the end. She took some kind of turn and went to her bed soon afterwards, refusing to get up even after the doctor came round and told her to do so. "Oh, he doesn't know," she'd say. "He hasn't got the foggiest notion of all the pain I'm going through." And then there'd be the shouts and yells from the bedroom. She even had a stick which she'd rap time and time again on the floor. "Oh, Neil, Neil!" she'd shout. "Won't you come round here quick? I need you right now." And I'd scurry away and try to attend her, having to leave customers behind in the shop. "Oh, excuse me!

Excuse me!" One of my customers told me that my shop was known as the one where coffee, flour and apologies were on offer every hour of the day. I had to laugh and agree with him. "Sorry about that," I said.'

'I've seen people in Tolsta like that,' Jessie said. 'They took to their beds and expected everyone around them to take up the burden.'

'Well, it had its own effect. When she passed away, the doctor told me she would have lived a lot longer if she'd have slipped out of the blankets a little more often. It didn't do her any good, all that lying around in bed.'

'I can imagine,' Jessie said, conscious for a moment that there were unfamiliar notes around, the sounds of small birds that could find shelter here among the nooks and crannies of strange trees but would be harried and blasted if they ever settled in the likes of Tolsta, their tiny quills and pinions flurried constantly by the wind. 'That must have been hard.'

'It was, sometimes. I think that's why I enjoyed so much writing and getting letters from you. It was different from getting one from my relatives. They would just mention what was happening to the family or the neighbours. Which one of them had died or passed away.'

'There's a lot like that.'

'Aye,' he grinned, sounding Scottish for a moment. 'No green shoots. Just the harvest.'

'It's a bit like that.'

'Well, your letters were very different. You seemed to notice everything that was going on around you. The changes that were taking place. It was as if you were trying to get me ready for the day I came back. You did think of that, didn't you?'

She took her time before answering, balancing every word on her tongue before she dared to speak it. She was assisted in this by the way a couple approached them with their dog on a lead. It was something she had never seen in Tolsta, where dogs were allowed to walk free most of the time, wandering from croft to croft, door to door. It always astonished her when she saw how they did not have quite the same freedom in town, the liberty to run around if they shied away from sheep, did not race upon the moor.

'I did. I thought there was a chance you might come back.'

'I thought that. You see, there's something I noticed when I was in Vermont. There's French women married to Scotsmen there, Swedes or Finns married to English women. Sometimes they're very happy together. Sometimes it's the right choice. Sometimes it's not.' He paused for a moment, a lark trilling above some green and treeless piece of land, a blackbird singing close to a thick, red-flowered bush. 'Yet I always think your chance of happiness increases if you're with someone who has a similar background to you, who can whisper to you in your own language. It's a way of bringing down barriers, opening borders. It's hard enough to explore the human heart without needing a lantern to help you look round it. And that's true even if people are both Scottish. It's the language itself – or the background – that's most important. The two of us share that.'

She felt herself grow giddy and reel, swaying like the top branches of nearby trees. The rustle of the unexpected. Whistling among leaves.

'What do you mean by that?' she asked.

* * *

It amazed Duncan how unsettled he was among familiar surroundings today. What did he mean by speaking to Ina that afternoon? Did he really want to take her to the dance tonight? How could he take her back to his home, be married and settled there? What could he do with his mother there?

His lack of ease showed almost the moment he arrived in Stornoway. The ignition keys slid from his hand after he parked the bus, spinning onto the ground and ending up just below the engine.

'Oh, damn,' he muttered, bending to try and scoop them up. Conscious he was wearing his smartest, neatest clothes, he took great care as he knelt to attempt to fetch them, his efforts earning the attention of an East Coast fisherman who was passing by.

'Ye've goat yersel in a richt fankle, lad!'

It was the same when he stepped into the Lido, ordering his usual coffee from Luigi behind the counter. This time it was coins that spun from his clutch; a sixpenny, a threepenny bit and a couple of pennies falling to the floor.

'You all right, Duncan?' Luigi asked.

'Aye. Just making a bit of a brochan of everything today.'

'We all have days like that,' Luigi smiled, his years in the town allowing him to understand the Gaelic word his customer had used, one that featured from time to time in his own conversation.

Duncan's grip was still clumsy as he made his way to the table near the window where his friends sat, spilling a little coffee into his saucer on the way.

'Suffering from dropsy?' Iain asked. 'You're not yourself today.'

'Aye… I wonder what's on your mind,' Roddy George asked, winking in the direction of the Town Hall on the opposite side of the street, a poster advertising tonight's dance emblazoned on its doors.

'It must be the football tonight,' he replied.

'Aye. You might tell yourself that, but you won't get off with telling the rest of us that story,' Roddy George laughed. 'We're not that easily fooled.'

He chuckled in response, his eye scanning the café to see who was there at that moment. There were a few old women from the countryside, each one talking while at the same time taking in each word their neighbours said. A few more East Coast fishermen than normal sat in their corner, deep in their usual conversation, talking of some test that was taking place. 'It shouldn't be happening,' one of them said. 'Not that close to land.' A few school-pupils were also perched beside one of the tables. So much was so familiar. The only unusual sight he had glimpsed that morning was a man dressed in the light, informal clothes that he imagined an American might wear, making his way from the Caledonian Hotel where he parked his bus. There was something about the dark, broad-shouldered man's stride that also caught Duncan's attention. His gait belonged to someone familiar with walking on the moorland, as if the pavement below his feet possessed the roll and dip of the terrain. It was a step that some people from the islands never lost, no matter where they travelled in their lives.

'Any idea what the result is going to be?' Roddy George asked.

Before he had any chance to answer, Ina and her friends came in the door. She blushed and smiled in his direction;

one of the girls close to her giggling. He trembled. Rising to his feet, his knee knocked against a table-leg. Roddy George laughed aloud, his coffee cup trembling on its surface.

'Where will we meet tonight?' Duncan stammered.

'At the Caley? Where you park your bus?'

'Aye. That'll be fine,' he said, before correcting himself. 'That'll be nice.'

He sat down once more, trying his best to be oblivious to the laughter and smirks that were going on all around him. He was assisted in this by the fact that a group of well-dressed men arrived at that moment. First of all, there were two of them – one a tall, dark, slightly distracted-looking young man accompanied by his shorter, fair-headed companion. Three others followed in their footsteps, making their way towards Luigi to order a coffee or tea.

'That must be them,' Duncan heard one of the fishermen say.

27

Stepping through the doors of the hotels and pubs, John looked at the beers on tap, the rows of bottles behind the counters, and recognised none of the labels. There was a bewildering variety of brands and kinds. Fowler's Wee Heavy. Youngers. McEwan's. Brown and Dark Ale. Forty Shilling. Sixty Shilling. Those premises decorated with a picture of some kind. Gentlemen with glasses, long white beards and grey hats, the slogan *Old Soldiers Never Die. They get YOUNGER every day* printed below. Bottles of Sweetheart Stouts with a young, fair-haired woman grinning enticingly in his direction. A tray advertising McEwan's Indian Pale Ale with a couple of flags spread out on its surface. Two soldiers wearing bearskins – one with a sweep of tartan over his shoulder and a kilt – swilling down a couple of glasses of beer. The legend McEwan's Beer Is Second To None.

And then there were the spirits. Dewar's Whisky. Watson's Trawler Rum with a fishing boat on its label – the Carella coming to his mind instantly, crashing its way through the waves. No sign of gin on offer. He could imagine Lillian declaring that there was nothing to drink here. Judging by the almost complete absence of women in these places, there were no females around to drink it either.

'I'll have two pints of bitter, please,' he said, nodding in the direction of Lambert as he spoke.

'What?' the barman asked. 'Sorry.'

'Two pints of bitter.'

'Oh, we don't have that here,' the barman smiled. 'Pint of heavy? Pint of mild?'

Dumbfounded, he shook his head. 'Any of the other places round here have it?'

'Bitter? No. Just heavy and mild.'

'Oh… Which is the one most like bitter?'

'I don't really know. Never tried bitter. How about heavy? That's the strongest one.'

John looked in Lambert's direction. 'What do you think?'

'Let's try it.'

His head reeling even before he sipped the drink, he took the two glasses with him to a table and sat down with his companion. He had barely touched it when the singing began. A gentleman in the far corner rose from his seat with a half pint of beer in one hand and a whisky in the other, swaying from side to side as the song echoed around the bar.

> 'Fàili, fàili, fàili ho ro
> Fàili, fàili, fàili ho ro
> Fàili, fàili, fàili ho ro,
> 'S cian nan cian on dh'fhàg mi Leòdhas...'

John shook his head, turning once again to Lambert.

'We have truly arrived in a foreign place,' he declared.

* * *

Jessie's head swirled in response to his question.

'Can I think about that?' she stammered. 'I need time to do that.'

* * *

'There's more folk coming here than the average Sunday going to church,' Roddy George said. 'Amazing number. All different ages.'

'It isn't often we get the chance to see a game like this,' Iain nodded.

'No doubt about that,' Duncan said, his eyes skirting the faces of the crowd who were filling Goathill Park. 'Not just locals, either. Quite a few of them are strangers.'

He recognised who some of them were, looking as strange and out of place as those he had seen in Gibraltar: the cockneys wearing kilts as they gathered in Casemates; one of the officers in his pyjamas chasing a Barbary ape that had entered and wrecked his apartment in the Castle Steps. Sometimes he himself had felt more than a little that way. One of the few outsiders who had ended up by chance in a regiment largely made up of men from Angus. The only Gaelic speaker among them.

The strangers here today were slightly less odd and uncomfortable than he had sometimes felt during the war. The monkey men off the *Ben Lomond*. A few fishermen from the East Coast boats. The man in the American clothes he had seen earlier, his outfit a little thin for the chill wind that was blowing across the park. There were more signs that he was a local, talking to a few men from Back as they stood on the edge of the pitch alongside the Lewis hospital. 'That's why the pitch is here,' someone had told him a while ago. 'If anyone goes down in a tackle, you can just lift them up and take them next door.' A moment or two later and, kitted out in blue and white, the Inverness team ran onto the pitch. Iain pointed out the ones he recognised as they appeared.

'Billy Pullar... Donnie Mackintosh... Ginger Mackenzie... Fast as any racehorse, that last one,' he declared. 'He could give them a run for their money at Ascot or Ayr.'

And then there came an even louder cheer, a clamour of handclaps. Duncan knew some of them. Dan MacAskill and Alex Macleod had been among his own passengers often over the years. Donald 'Safety' Smith. Torquil Macleod. 'Stoodie' Mackay. Iain made sure that the two Carloway team members were pointed out.

'Larry Maciver. Marco Macdonald. They're quality!'

'What? You're only saying that because they come from your part of the island!' Roddy George laughed. 'The only good thing about there is the Callanish Stones. They've got a lot in common with the rest of the population: stuck in the past and unable to shift.'

'Hoi! The trouble is that the only thing that's quick about you is your tongue.'

Duncan grinned as he listened, picking out some of the others playing. Hughie Davidson. Dol Angie Macdonald. The Gaelic singer who spent much of his life driving a bus from Stornoway to his home-district of Point, John 'Hoddan' Macdonald, a broad-shouldered man with swept-back hair.

'Make sure you turn *cuibhle an fhortain* on them,' someone from the ground yelled, referring to one of his Gaelic songs. 'Roll them down.'

And then someone began to sing the song's opening lines:

'Tha cuibhle an fhortain ri cur nan caran;
'S gur mise dh'fhairich siud ged is òg mi.'

'The wheel of fortune – it keeps on turning.
I know that well even though I'm young.'

Hoddan laughed in response, pressing his finger against his lips.

'*Isd*,' he grinned, telling them to hush.

The song was brought to an end by the referee blowing the whistle for the game to start, bringing the ball to its centre. By that time, however, Duncan's attention was already wandering. He could see Ina with two of her friends on the far side of the pitch, standing near the Inverness Caledonian goal. He nodded towards her, pleased that she blushed and grinned back. Her response made him bolder, aware that even Iain and Roddy George's attention was – like everyone else – focused on the game. Taking advantage of this, he mouthed some words in her direction.

'Fancy going for a walk?'

She grinned again and nodded; the word 'yes' shaped on her lips.

He found the opportunity a few moments later to slip away from his friends, aware too that she was performing a similar action, heading in the direction of the entrance to the ground. He could not help smiling as he did this. There was no doubt that the *cuibhle an fhortain* was turning a little like the tyres of the buses both he and Hoddan drove – slowly and to his advantage.

28

There was a woman serving in one of the pubs. John didn't know which one it was. He had lost all sense of that long ago, somewhere between the County Hotel and the Carlton Bar, Mac's Imperial and the Star Inn. A few pints and whiskies back, after Lambert, too, had gone and disappeared on him. All he was aware of now was that the woman's movements and gestures were familiar. The way she dipped glasses into soapy water. Filled pints at the beer taps. Stood before a clock that was set five minutes too fast. Spoke to visitors and regulars with an intense look of interest on her face. Accepted coins pressed into her palm with a smile. Flirted as she moved between bar and tables. All that was something way too familiar to him.

And there was the way she looked. The red daub of lipstick. The way a cigarette dangled from her fingers. Her long, black hair loose upon her shoulders. Knitted dress, not unlike the pale blue one he had seen her wear before. The necklace hanging round her neck. The light and energy in her eyes. *Boom!* And Lillian was in there, her face a little blurred and different, within the lounge of the Talbot Inn once more, listening to Billy the Lip talk about the achievements of Bury FC or Preston North End, smiling at the young men and their feeble attempts at jokes.

'You remind me of someone,' John told the woman, drawing her towards him with a wriggle of his finger.

'Oh?'

'Yes. Someone I love very much.'

His feet slipped from him once again as he leaned on the counter. He felt his balance go, almost falling to the floor. He held on, grasping the counter with his fingers.

'I want to tell you something,' he began. 'What happened to that boat from your home-town, that made me change my mind. Made me realise that what we were doing to monkeys and guinea pigs was not right… Not meant to poison your people. Not meant to poison them at all.'

'Sorry?'

'No. It was an accident. Wasn't meant to happen.' His voice slurred and slithered, trying to keep some sort of grip on vowels and consonants. 'These people… They just blundered their way through the gas… They just…'

He stopped, aware of the look of bemusement on the young woman's face. She looked nothing like Lillian. Her features were softer, rounder. Her brown eyes were puzzled and perplexed.

'Oh God,' he said. 'What have I gone and told you? What have I gone and done?'

He turned around, stumbling out of the pub, past customers playing dominoes at a table, a young couple whispering in the corner of the bar. He nearly knocked against them, making his way out the door.

'Oh God…' he kept mumbling. 'Oh God… Oh God … Oh God.'

As he stepped outside into the twilight, he nearly knocked against someone who was making his way down the street. Looking up, he saw it was one of the local ministers. He was wearing a Homburg hat, a dog-collar around his neck, and a thick, grey coat.

'Sorry… Sorry… Sorry,' he mumbled.

'That's all right,' the minister replied. 'Accidents will happen.'

'Yes. Yes. They will,' John muttered, the man's presence reminding him of that time Lillian had opened the Bible in front of him, the words she had read: '*And in that day will I make a covenant for them with the beasts of the field and with the fowls of heaven, and with the creeping things of the ground…*'

'Oh, God,' he mumbled again. 'Oh, God. Oh God. Oh God.'

* * *

It was only in the quiet of her bedroom that Jessie began to make sense of the conversation that had occurred that afternoon – how Neil had asked her if she'd ever thought of going to America after that time, taking one of the boats – the *Marloch* or *Canada* – going to Saint John, New Brunswick, or beyond.

'Not after George disappeared. There seemed to be no point. It would have been like chasing after a ghost.'

'And it never came to your mind again – not even after others left the district?'

'No.' She shook her head. 'No. I just settled down to do what I'm still doing today. Worked with the sheep. The croft. The peats. Walked to the moor and shore when I wanted to be alone, feel no one's eyes on me.'

'And that happens often?'

'Yes,' she said, feeling unsettled by his question. 'If you're in a wee village like Tolsta, you have to get away from it from time and time.'

'It's even true in Williamstown sometime,' Neil smiled.

'I suppose it's true of any small places,' she said. 'People wanting to know all your business. Even making it up at times.'

'Aye. Again, that's true in the New World as well as the Old.'

She nodded, aware that the more he spoke, the more his Hebridean accent was returning. His voice was softening, losing its slightly nasal edge, recapturing the lilt he possessed in his youth. With each day that passed while he stayed on the island, it was more likely that his speech would blend in with his neighbours, making it impossible to tell the difference between him and the others in Upper Coll, his years in Vermont almost forgotten.

'Would you ever think of coming back home?' she asked.

'Me? I do it all the time. Never a night goes back when I don't think about the chance of doing so. But it's not practical. I have a business to run over there. Someone's helping me to do that at the moment, but I can't stay here too long. It can only be done for a little while. Only a month or so.'

'That must be disappointing for you.'

'Aye. But I hope to bring something of home with me. Back to Vermont.'

Her footsteps stilled. A blackbird was swirling and dipping around a statue that had been sculpted a short distance away. She noticed there were poppies carved on top of the pillars that stood around it – a reminder of the trade that had provided wealth to the man who had built these grounds centuries ago. She recalled George once talking about how the town was tainted by this, the way that the builder of the castle had profited from a plague he and his kind had unleashed on the Chinese people centuries before. 'We should be ashamed of every tree that stands there,' he had said. 'Bitterly ashamed.' Again she tried to wash the thought from her head. That had all been so long before, her long wait for him a waste of the years of her youth.

'I've got an idea to put to you,' Neil said. 'One that you might think is a little daft or crazy. Would you fancy coming over to Vermont for a month or two, perhaps – if you like it – even longer?'

Her face coloured. 'What do you mean?'

It was his turn to stammer. 'I didn't mean to move in with me,' he explained. 'You could move in first with Jock and Avis. They have a spare room. It would give you time to get used to Vermont, spending time too with fellow islanders. Get used to me. We both deserve a chance of happiness. Of creating a new life for ourselves.'

Her breath faltered in the weight of his words. She felt herself unable to speak.

'What do you think?' he asked.

Her head swirled. 'Can I think about that?' she stammered. 'I need time to do that.'

∗ ∗ ∗

Duncan did not believe he had ever driven the bus more quickly, aware that he had to turn it around and head back to Stornoway and see Ina again, going with her to the dance. He barely heard the conversation of his passengers, only being aware that the Lewis Select side had drawn three–all with their Highland opponents, that Stoodie had scored two of the goals and Torquil Macleod – or 'Blake' – had scored the other one.

'A great game. A great game,' Shonnie, one of his passengers, had said. 'Where were you? I didn't see you at it.'

'Oh. Other things got in the way,' he declared.

He was lucky he didn't need to answer more than that. One of the lads sitting at the back was paying his own tribute to Hoddan, singing the song for which he was best known.

'Tha cuibhle an fhortain ri cur nan caran;
'S gur mise dh'fhairich siud ged is òg mi.'

Duncan was thinking all the time of Ina, and how they had walked round Stornoway together, circling the town during the time the game was being played. They had gone down Goathill Road and Church Street, stepping over the length of Cromwell Street before climbing up the road again, past St Martin's Memorial, the school and the High Church. As they did this, she talked of her parents and brother, how she was set to inherit a croft in the village of Crossbost where a maiden aunt stayed. How, too, she had been watching him for a long time as he sat in the Lido Café. It was the reason, she said, she always went there instead of anywhere else.

'I kept wondering when you might ask me out,' she said. 'I must admit I had almost given up hope. Didn't think you even noticed me when I came in.'

'Oh… I most certainly did,' he grinned. 'Every single time.'

'I think I know that now,' she laughed.

What he didn't tell her was about the doubts he suffered, how he didn't want to take her to a house that was occupied by his mother; how – despite his ease with others – he felt shy and tongue-tied when he tried to speak to young women around his age; how there were moments when, because of this, he had an almost physical sensation that he had allowed his youth to slip away from him, never quite obtaining a grasp on life.

But there would be other times when he would have the chance to talk of these things.

Just now, there was the prospect of the dance.

29

John decided to head in the direction of the music he could hear a short distance away. It was not the Big Band sound he had heard time and time again in English cities. Not Ted Heath and His Music. Not the Billy Cotton Big Band. Not the Squadronaires. Not music like *Somebody Stole My Gal*. Not the *South Rampart Street Parade* or *There's Something In The Air* or the tunes of Glenn Miller. This sounded nothing like that. No trumpet. No saxophone. No brass. Instead, there was the jagged rhythm of the accordion, a hoot and holler from those inside, the stamp of feet, clap of hands. Tunes he could not begin to understand.

Despite this, he decided to make his way towards it, aware that his friends and companions were probably there, as they had been at the football earlier. He swayed from side to side of the street, leaning for a moment on the window of the Lido before he stepped towards the doors. He braced himself as he did this, conscious he had to appear more sober than he actually felt. Checking his appearance one more time, he made his way into the hall, pushing past its heavy wooden doors, fumbling with change to pay his ticket.

And then he was in there, among all the accordions, guitar and drum-kit noises, the hubbub and cheer that was echoing all round. He could see them all in the sudden brightness – Lambert, Mackay, Harvey, Wilson – standing at the edge of the dancers, nodding their heads as he entered. There were others, too, a motley crew inside the hall. The fishermen he had seen in the harbour the other day, their waterproofs forsaken in favour of smart clothes. The man he'd noticed in the Lido earlier, his gaze continually flicking in the direction of the girl he had seen at the counter. She was with him this time, a shyness about them that showed they were not quite at ease with each other. Other women circled near them, as if they were talking with one another, sharing secrets about a relationship they had not yet grasped or understood. He was conscious, too, that some were glancing in his direction. Whether out of admiration or in horror at his drunken condition, he could not quite grasp. It didn't matter. '*Bibo ergo sum*,' he remembered a Latin student among his schoolfriends declaring. 'I drink, therefore I am.'

'Take your partners for the Gay Gordons,' he heard the guitarist on stage announce.

He watched them move around the hall. Lambert and Harvey approaching one of the local girls. Mackay, too, looking more comfortable than he often did on board the *Ben Lomond* following in their footsteps. Some of the fishermen were behaving the same way, frowning and muttering if one of John's shipmates managed to reach their planned destination before them. The young man with the tweed jacket was also guiding his partner onto the floor, smiling shyly as he did so. And then there were those who were content to sit down, cradling Capstans in their fingers, the bulge of a half-bottle apparent in their inside pockets. Sometimes they would stub their cigarettes in the ashtray before heading to the toilet or outdoors for a drink.

And once again it was in there. He was no longer in Stornoway but somewhere else. A dance-hall in Fleetwood, perhaps. The Blackpool Tower ballroom, with its chandeliers and decorated ceilings. One in Liverpool or Manchester. The fishermen on the *Carella* dressed up in their best clothes, like the ones here, to link with their partners' hands, drape arms around shoulders, take step by measured, rhythmic step alongside one another. Fingers touching. The women twirling round and round. Their breath mingling with each other as they circled and spun. Inhale. Exhale. That poison drawn into one another's lungs. The plague passed on. One step. Two step. Vomiting. Choking. Gasping for breath. They all fall down. Among them, he could even see the young woman from the bar. She had been flirting with customers in the same way Lillian did, nodding at the words of those like Billy the Lip who spoke to her. It was all like a nightmare swirling round his head.

What could he do? It was all so obvious to him. The vapour of the gas he had seen trailing across the pontoon near Tolsta Head as apparent to him as the veil of cigarette smoke that hung around this hall. The jackets and scarves piled on chairs coated with it, as surely as on the dead bodies of monkeys and guinea pigs washed up on that beach. It soaked and stained shirts and blouses, became trapped in hair and skin. It moved forward with every step of the dance they were taking, each note that the accordionist played. Soon it would not only be here – but in the streets these people walked, the houses they visited, the factories and fish-markets where some of their lives were spent. He saw it even in the catches they were handling, even the pots and pans they were boiled and cooked within. It was if the words 'Operation Cauldron' had taken on an entirely different meaning. Each stir of a spoon, gurgle of steam, helping that plague and pestilence to spread. Hubble, bubble, toil and trouble…

'Stop it! Stop it!' he shouted. 'Do you know what you're doing? Do you have any idea?'

He stepped forward, colliding against one of the young women who was dancing at the edge of the group. She stumbled, falling to the floor. The next thing he was aware of was a man staring at him, rolling up his sleeves.

'What the hell are you up to?'

It was chaos after that – the blow to his face, knocking him to the ground, the start of a thousand other fights. The East Coast fishermen against their island counterparts. Those from the *Ben Lomond* against both groups. One punch following another. One kick preceding the next. The women screaming, except for the few who also joined in, tugging hair, using teeth and nails to bite and scratch. The accordionist still pounding his instrument, pushing keys, his music sounding more disjointed and desperate the longer the fight went on.

* * *

Jessie was still restless, still unable to sleep. She tried to blame other things for this – the corncrake in a nearby field of oats that was sending out a loud, persistent signal for a partner, the weeping sound of a curlew as it swept overhead – but she knew in herself that it had much to do with her own state of mind, the dilemma in which she had found herself. Finally, she put on her dressing gown and slippers and went down to the kitchen to make herself a cup of tea. She felt she resembled the moth that appeared in the room the moment the tilly lamp began to glow. It flitted between the curtains and the edge of the stove, still warm even if it had lost a little of the evening's heat. With its tufted black-and-white wings circling the room continually, touching down before lifting off almost immediately afterwards, the moth was like the workings of her mind, unable to settle, to properly consider or contemplate things, trembling as vigorously as her heart had done ever since that walk with Neil in the castle grounds.

There were so many thoughts cramming her head. The letters she had read from people in the village who said that moving to either Canada or the States had been the best thing they had ever done in their life. Angus who had written that moving to Portland in Oregon had been the best thing he had ever done in his life. *I never have to worry about lacking money here*, he said. *There's always a few coins jingling in my pocket. It wasn't always like that at home.* There were those, too, who never looked back, setting up businesses for themselves in places like Massachusetts, Toronto, Calgary. There were no letters from them. Just whispers of how prosperous they were, how wealthy they had become. She heard about them, quiet boasts from the lips of neighbours and relatives.

'Oh, they're doing awfully well...'

And then there were those like Mairead's man, Donald Gillies, from Skigersta, who had shuffled back home again with scraped and broken soles, unable to cope with life in the New World once the Great Depression had arrived, sweeping away the industries in which they had worked. There were a few, of course, whose problems had not been so extreme. People like Murdo Macfarlane, who in his song *Fàili, fàili, fàili ho ro* had complained there were no ceilidhs to be found on the prairie, noting how much he pined for the sound of waves on the shore. He wasn't alone in that. There were others who left their home and mourned the absence of an *Eilean Beag Donn a' Chuain* from their existence, yearning for its presence each day of their lives. Who knows? Her own George might have been among them, missing those with whom he had shared his days before that voyage had taken him away from these shores. He had probably done so from the instant he had first encountered people from other places on the *Metagama*. The strangeness of their prayers alarming him; the differences between their voices and his own.

Would she be content if she moved across to Williamstown, especially at this stage of her life?

It might mean freedom for her, the chance to walk in the shade of branches and trees, and not to be forever watched on moor and shore.

Would she survive that far from home?

She didn't know the answer to that one. Sipping her tea, she sang to herself as she always did on those rare nights she could not sleep, the very tunes and words she had sung with Mairead for many years, the two of them old and long-term friends. She missed her now. She would be the very person she could speak to about her problem – another woman who had wasted her youth dreaming of an absent man, one that like her own had sung the same song before he booked his passage on the *Metagama*, dreaming, perhaps, of the Rockies or the Appalachian hills.

An tèid thu leam, a rìbhinn òg,
A rìbhinn òg, a rìbhinn òg,

Sèist

An tèid thu leam, a rìbhinn òg,
A-null gu tìr nam beanntan?

Will you go with me, my young maid,
My young maid, my young maid,
Will you go with me, my young maid
Over to the land of mountains?

A few things had, however, changed since then. The lines on her face reminded her that she was no longer young as she had been when George had serenaded her with those words. Instead, too, of being a land filled with mountains, it was now a landscape where the earth was shadowed by trees she was being asked to make her way towards.

* * *

'That was a lot more explosive than I expected,' Duncan grinned as he and Ina stood together in front of the bus.

'A lot!' Ina laughed, 'I don't suppose many first dates turn out like that.'

'Not unless they go very badly wrong. I hope it wasn't too much of a disappointment.'

'Not at all,' she grinned. 'I'm just wondering how you're going to follow it. You'll have to try and make it even more spectacular next time.'

'There are other ways of doing that,' he said.

He decided to kiss her, faltering as he did so, his whole body quaking as he geared up for the movement. She responded to him in much the same way, eager and clumsy as their lips met.

'That's another way of being explosive,' she giggled. 'Try it again. See if we can set off some fireworks.'

'I'll do my best.'

It was a more convincing kiss this time, a sure and certain embrace. He kissed her with an intensity and confidence he was surprised to find in himself; aware, too, that she responded in much the same way, the entire experience making him shake and tremble.

'Will I see you tomorrow?'

'No. I can't. I promised Mam and Dad I'd go and help in the peats.'

'Monday?'

'Of course. Monday. In the Lido.'

'Yes. We can even sit together.'

'Oh, that'll be a bit explosive,' she laughed. 'But I'm sure we can manage it.'

'It would be a nice change.'

'It certainly would be.'

They kissed once again, their bodies coming together. They broke apart a moment later when they became aware of a man shuffling towards them, leaning from time to time on the side of the bus. It was clear from the manner in which he stumbled that he had consumed a lot more than he should have. Despite this, he wandered on, heading towards the cars parked a short distance away at the Fisherman's Mart. He tugged at the door of one a few times before turning away, moving to the next vehicle. A dramatic lurch before he succeeded in opening this car door, pulling at the handle and clambering into the driver's seat.

'There's a chance of something spectacular happening there,' Ina whispered.

'Especially if he goes home like that to his wife.'

They kissed again, enjoying the warmth and strength of each other, how their breath and flesh laced together. They barely heard the car starting a short distance away, failed to notice how the driver didn't put on the headlights. The vehicle revved a little too much as it moved away.

'Another explosion,' Duncan laughed.

'Yes… There seem to be a lot of them about tonight.'

Just as their lips came into contact again, they heard the shouting.

'Ina! Ina! We're heading off home!'

The young woman's voice was followed by the shout of a man.

'Come on, Ina! Don't dilly-dally any longer! If you do, we'll have to head off without you! It's a hell of a long way to walk!'

30

John was lucky the road was empty. Leaving Stornoway, he felt the car lurch occasionally, striking the edge of the pavement, veering towards a grass verge, scattering chippings from the surface of the road. He gripped the steering wheel tighter, trying to get away from the trouble he had caused in the town, aware that his job wasn't safe any longer, that his marriage too was in danger of coming to an end. Even what he had blurted out in the bar might be a breach of the Official Secrets Act. If the barmaid had made any kind of sense of his ramblings… If she talked to the police or the authorities…

All deep, deep shit.

He had no idea where he was travelling, just vague thoughts of heading to the place he had heard them speaking about – that stretch of sand, the bridge to nowhere, perhaps, somewhere he could fade away, a shack on the moorland where he might hide and disappear for a time until all the hubbub had died down. If it ever did. There would be fish and rabbits he could eat. A moorland bird or two he could feed upon. Not that he knew anything about them. Not that he knew much about anything, really. Apart from his job. Apart from using testing equipment. Cleaning beakers and syringes, funnels, flasks and Petri dishes, the array of glass that was used inside the lab. It would take a lot more than soap and water to clean his flesh and mind after this one, much more than a quick rinse in the sink, a dip in the Minch.

Hell! A long swerve ahead into the darkness. He gripped the wheel tight again, feeling it slip once more from his fingers. His head was spinning even more than the tyres. His eyes were opening and closing continually. And all the time Lillian's face was coming into his head, telling him how wrong she thought his job was, the killing of animals for science. 'We have no right to treat them that way. No right whatsoever.' And that was only the half of it. She didn't have a clue what he and his kind had unleashed on Fleetwood. The gases swirling around unnoticed in the darkness. The gleam of either of the town's lighthouses unable to shine any light on the presence of what the *Carella* had brought to its piers and fish-market, its population unaware as it shifted from one person to the next, one grip to another, slipping easily through handshakes, kisses, slaps on the back. Passed on like some infernal parcel, one that was packed and filled with death and illness, plague and pestilence.

He revved the car again, as if in doing this, he could drive away quickly and clear all these thoughts from his head.

* * *

The corncrake had won. Jessie heard its croak again and again, echoing across the houses and crofts of Tolsta. This was always the most difficult time of year to sleep here. The bleat of sheep. The constant birdsong. Larks. Starlings. Thrushes. The birds – like the terns with their loud screeches – that had travelled halfway across the world in search of the perpetual light which often left her tired and sleepless, exhausted during much of the day. 'Seasonal insomnia,' she had heard one of the doctors call it. 'The curse of northern climes at this time of year.' She wondered if there would be much change in that if she ever went to stay in Williamstown with Neil. How far north was Vermont? From her memory, it seemed to be close to Canada. She imagined that there might be the same kind of hours of daylight there during the summer months. Birds – with names she could neither imagine or know – would sweep and sing within that landscape, nesting in the branches of trees, filling up the forest with their own distinctive notes and cries, keeping her awake.

And then there would be the winter.

She wondered how cruel that season would be there. It was hard enough here with its salt-laden winds, the storms that sometimes lasted for days on end. She had read in one of the letters home about a man from Vatisker who had settled in Dawson City in the far north; how deep the snow would lie there, often making it impossible for anyone to venture into the main street for weeks. There were countless tales of men fastening traditional Canadian snowshoes – Bearpaw, Huron, Ojibwe – to make their way through the ardours of the winter. One story told of how the door of someone's house had been blocked by the weight of snow, trapping them within their home for days.

'We lit a fire with logs on the stone floor beside it, hoping it would melt away the ice. The smoke from it nearly choked us.'

She had heard songs, too, in which exiles bemoaned their new lives in places like Manitoba, where some of her fellow Hebrideans had been encouraged to journey towards. There was one, written by someone from Uist, which she and Mairead had sometimes sang during the nights they spent together.

Thig iad thugainn, carach, seòlta
Gus ar mealladh far ar n-eòlais
Molaidh iad dhuinn Manitòba
Dùthaich fhuar gun ghual gun mhòine.

They will come to us, cunning, wily,
In order to entice us from our homes.
They will praise Manitoba to us,
A cold land without coal or peat.

She wondered if Neil was also doing that, praising Vermont and all its wonders, hoping to entice her from her native village only for her to discover – like that songwriter from Uist – that she would miss these surroundings in the end. Perhaps, though, this was her natural distrust, one that had started with George and his broken promises all those years before. Perhaps it was the way she doubted herself, that any man would want her at this stage in her life.

As this thought travelled through her mind, she heard the crash outside.

* * *

Driving through the Gleann Mhor, Duncan could see the car in front of him, swerving from side to side even within the tight parameters of that road. He could see it narrowly miss a sheep grazing on the verge, weaving its way around it in the twilight, continuing its direction north. He could tell its driver was drunk, for all that he didn't recognise the vehicle that was careening at a faster speed than was safe along that slope. Someone from town, perhaps? A stranger to the community?

Watching as it wavered, he relived the nightmare that was often in his head since that day the bomb had nearly struck his lorry near South Barrack Square. He imagined the car ahead of him toppling down the slope, turning again and again, bouncing against grass, rock and heather till it ended up upside down or upright, perhaps upon its side. A windscreen being smashed. Metal torn and dented. Blood and glass. The gash of an open wound. Its redness staining seats and crumpled dashboard. The gasp of breath until it died out, coming to an end.

Duncan pushed down on the accelerator, shifting gears, following that car to the outside of the village, where the crash occurred.

* * *

Jessie reached the car first. It had collided with the wall of a barn a short distance from her home. She raced across the road in dressing gown and wellingtons, finding a man inside the vehicle, groaning and sobbing as he lay sprawled across the seat. His face was lashed with blood, his fingers prickled with broken fragments and splinters. Around him, there was the stink of piss and booze. In the background, she could hear hens, clucking and squawking in alarm.

'Help,' he muttered. 'Help.'

Almost as he said this, the bus pulled up. Duncan clambered out of it, looking alarmed and frightened.

'Go and get Mairead!' Jessie yelled. 'She's good at this kind of thing. After that, get the nurse, the hospital and police.'

White-faced, Duncan nodded, climbing into his bus again.

'Is this the bridge?' the man kept saying. 'Have I reached the bridge yet?'

31

It was a place John never expected to be in, this building with its varnished doors and cream-painted walls, the colour of a prison cell. Stornoway's Sheriff Court, on a day when mist shrouded the town. He looked across the room at the judge with his white wig. Shepherd was speaking on John's behalf, talking about his good character and reputation, the fact that he had never let them down in all the years he had been employed by them.

'There's no doubt in my mind that John Anthony Herrod is a decent and honourable man. He has shown that during all the time he has worked for us. Punctual. Dedicated. Capable of great understanding and excellent ideas. There has never been a previous occasion when either his attitude or work-rate has been affected by either the consumption of alcohol or his private life. He has given his all to us as his employers. This is what has made this incident – no, this succession of incidents – all the more surprising to us. None of this fits with our conception and impression of the man. One can only ask questions. He is fairly newly married. He moved down in recent years from his old home in the north-west of England to Salisbury. Perhaps it is these adjustments that have had an effect on him. However, there is no doubt in my mind that he is genuinely shocked and remorseful about all that he has done here in this town. He asks this court for your forgiveness and mercy when his sentence is handed out. I have no doubt he has learned a valuable lesson from all that has occurred.'

And then there was another flurry of words. John looked down at his lacerated fingers, conscious too of the scars on his face as the judge spoke, his words echoing round the court-room. He bowed his head and waited for his sentence.

* * *

Neil and Jessie sat together by the window of the Lido Café, looking out at the notice fixed to the Town Hall door. It declared, by order of the Town Council, that no further dances would be held 'until further notice'.

'I've heard that there was a big fight there the other night, between the Buckie men and the local fishermen. Among all the jigs and reels. That's why they put that notice up.'

'Nothing's changed then,' Jessie said. 'My father told me that used to go on years ago. In fact, much worse.'

'Aye. My dad told me that, too. Never trust a Bucach.'

After that, they drained their coffees, going round the corner to Francis Street to get away from people. The way the gaze of some people from Back or Gress fell on them. One or two young women from the tweed factory. They climbed the foot of the hill, past the shops and stores there. Reaching the foot of Martin's Memorial Church, Neil turned towards her.

'Well? Will you go across to Vermont?'

She paused before responding. She had been all too aware for days that this moment lay before her, for all that she had never envisaged it taking place in the shade of this building, a short distance from the steps where she and George had stood some thirty years before.

'No,' she said.

Sighing, he shook his head. 'May I ask you why?'

'Yes,' she nodded. 'You can. I belong here. I'm part of this landscape. Those people I know here are my friends, those with whom I have shared my life. It's familiar to me. Twenty years ago, I may have been able to make other friends, get to know the secrets of those trees you were talking about. But it's too late now. Impossible to make that change.'

'You sure? You could try.'

'It would be a huge effort,' she smiled. 'And it's one I wouldn't be prepared to make for the sake of the next twenty years or so. It'll be enough to be battling against rheumatism, arthritis – things people normally suffer from in old age. Not starting a new life.'

'Oh, well…'

He looked downcast, his face crumpling. His feet reeled a little, as though he had consumed a glass of beer or whisky too many. He shuddered before he spoke again.

'Oh well…' he repeated, drawing breath once more. 'Can I give you a kiss for old times?'

'Do you really want to?' she said, looking around carefully to make sure there was no one about who recognised her.

'Yes. At least it would mean I took away a souvenir of my time at home.'

'Oh, all right then.'

She closed her eyes as he bowed his head towards her, feeling his lips upon hers. Clumsy, short and virginal – it was a flurry and brush with the promise of another, different life, sharpened and made sad by her memory of an earlier time, another moment of affection that had taken place before the church tower.

'Goodbye,' she said as he moved away. 'Goodbye.'

* * *

Duncan and Ina did not go to the Lido that day.

Instead, they sat on the bench in the castle grounds together, sharing sandwiches and a vacuum flask filled with tea, listening to the music of the birds perched on the branches around them, enjoying the new and different landscape they had discovered.

Open the door now.
Go roll up the collar of your coat
to walk in the changing scarf of mist.'

'Pearl Fog',
Carl Sandburg (1878–1967)

Inspirations
Dark and Light

For all that it is based on fact, *In A Veil of Mist* has much of its basis in the myths, half-truths and whispers that surrounded the coming of the *Ben Lomond* to the shores of the Isle of Lewis in May 1952.

It spawned a hundred legends. Even while I wrote this book, I heard a number of new stories connected with Operation Cauldron, even though it took place decades ago. One person claimed that he had seen the *Carella* a short distance from his home village, trailing white mist and being followed by a number of other vessels near one of the island's headlands. Another told me they had heard about cattle dying near the beach in Tolsta, victims of the poisonous gases swirling around the pontoon close to its shore. Some argued that there had been a series of deaths linked to cancer in the village caused by the various experiments that had occurred.

And then there were my own misunderstandings, which I have left unchecked and unchanged in the novel. They include the notion that the corpses of monkeys and guinea pigs were washed up on the beach, and the idea that the *Carella* was travelling south to its home port of Fleetwood when the incident occurred. It wasn't. Instead, it was heading north to Icelandic waters. The trawler was followed there by a fishery protection vessel and others, and continually checked for unpredictable and erratic movements while it fished. The same was done for a few weeks after the *Carella*'s return; the health, welfare and actions of its crew watched constantly during this time.[1]

With the exception of this last one, I have no idea if any of these stories are false or true. Neither have I made any attempts to check, convincing myself – rightly or wrongly – that in the context of a fictional work, it was okay to allow the myths to stand. (This is clearly not the case with a factual work.) I can even add my own half-truth to the brew, one that has been bubbling away in my head since I first heard of Operation Cauldron way back when. In essence, this novel was engendered by a short report I recall reading in the annals of the *Stornoway Gazette* many years ago. One of many 'wee stories from the police courts' that featured in its pages, it concerned an incident that took place involving a member of staff from the *Ben Lomond* while undertaking a visit to the island. The details of this are hazy in my mind, but I do recall that a senior officer declared the individual's actions to be entirely out of character. He had always been decent, honest and reliable before. Together with another faint recollection – an account of the banning of late-night dances in Stornoway Town Hall in the early Fifties due to fights occurring in the building – the genesis of *In a Veil of Mist* came into my head.

---

[1] Lewis and Harris football supporters will even note that I got the date of the football match between Inverness Caledonian and the Lewis Select 'wrong'. This occurred in early July 1952. The *Carella* incident took place on 16th September 1952. For dramatic reasons, I placed them in the wrong order. Nor am I sure exactly when the visit of the Stornoway dignitaries to the vessel happened, or who exactly was in the party. The *Ben Lomond* was off Tolsta between May and December of 1952. The visit occurred at some time during this period.

Yet for all that this book is fiction, it is also important to recall its basis in fact. Following the abandonment of the development of chemical weapons after their use (and abuse) in the First World War, Britain began to experiment once again in this field in the late thirties, stockpiling mustard gas and other gases in a new factory in Sutton Oak, St Helens, Lancashire (now Merseyside). Mustard gas was, for instance, tested in Hampshire, where its effects were seen to linger on sand and shingle, prompting Churchill to ponder the possibility of lacing British beaches with it to prevent a German invasion at the outbreak of World War Two.

All this was prompted by Italian actions in the invasion of Abyssinia (or Ethiopia) in 1935. They spray-bombed much of that country, creating a continuous fog that polluted rivers and lakes, causing people to suffer effects such as peeling skin, vomiting, an inability to walk and, eventually, death by asphyxiation. British scientists were also acutely aware that other nations were following their example. They included Nazi Germany, the Soviet Union and the Japanese. By the mid-Forties, the United Kingdom was building up stocks of such deadly concoctions as mustard, phosgene, tear gas and BBC (bromobenzyl cyanide) at locations like Porton Down and Sutton Oak, under 'conditions of extreme secrecy and urgency'.

Another aspect of this approach was the perceived need to identify which infectious illnesses could be used in airborne weapons and sprays as a way of releasing their micro-organisms on the enemy. One of these was anthrax, a highly contagious disease that kills animals, especially cattle and sheep, but is also fatal to humans, causing a hideous cancer among those with whom it comes into contact. It was this substance that was used in the island of Gruinard near Aultbea off the west coast of Ross and Cromarty, which is now part of Highland region. Bombs containing anthrax were dropped on the island, as described within the pages of this book. Capable of mass killing, this biological weapon was said to be 1,000 times more effective than its chemical equivalent. But there were issues with it as an instrument of death. It remained in the island soil for generations, and the testing may have been responsible for three minor outbreaks of anthrax that took place in 1954, 1961 and 1965. Gruinard was only 'cleansed' and returned to the descendants of its original owners in 1990. Peculiarly, since completing this novel, I have also discovered that two of the places mentioned in its pages, Blackpool Tower and Porton Down, also possibly played a role in this 'cleansing' of the island. In 1981, an extreme Scottish independence group, called the Dark Harvest Commando, left small mounds of contaminated soil from an area of the mainland near Gruinard beside Porton Down and the foot of Blackpool Tower. These acts were done when the Conservative party was holding its annual conference in that seaside town. This may be one of the reasons that the government began its decontamination programme later that decade.

It was partly the errors associated with the Gruinard experience that led to the next round of trials being associated with the sea. Collectively known as Pandora, these were conducted on floating laboratories on board two former tank-landing ships, HMS *Ben Lomond* and HMS *Narvik,* converted in order to house staff from Porton Down and also to take on board a large stock of animals. There were five of these trials in a seven-year period in the late Forties and Fifties. The first,

Operation Harness, is mentioned in this book. It occurred off the Bahamas to determine 'the practicality of sea trials' to test bacterial agents. The next two both involved the waters off the isle of Lewis. These were Operation Cauldron and its successor, Operation Hesperus. The final tests – Operation Ozone and Operation Negation – occurred again near the coastline of the Bahamas.[2] Like Cauldron and Hesperus, these experiments were joint operations with the United States and Canadian military. After the final test in 1955, both the vessels deployed for this purpose were taken to a naval dockyard and broken up. As a result of their use in these tests, they could not be employed in any other way.

Much of the information we possess about the *Carella* and Operation Cauldron we owe to the late Clive Ponting, who died in July 2020. Known as the civil servant who was the whistle-blower revealing details about the sinking of the Argentinian cruiser *General Belgrano* during the Falklands war, he was also the individual who leaked the details of the incident involving the *Carella* to the *Observer* newspaper in 1984. He did this after discovering a highly classified file on the topic in a Ministry of Defence safe. The story appeared under the headline 'British Germ Bomb Sprayed Trawler' in July 1985.

The account also reveals that the only reason the crew of the *Carella* survived the encounter was because the method of spreading and circulating the virus employed by those on the *Ben Lomond* failed to work.

---

[2] Interestingly, in our current context, both these last tests involved not only checking the efficacy of spraying agents but also the practicality of using a virus as a weapon.

For all that we now look back and question the motivation and thinking behind Operation Cauldron, there is little evidence that many did at the time. As some of the characters declare in the pages of *In a Veil of Mist*, they had experienced the opening days – and before – of World War Two and knew that the United Kingdom had been unprepared for that conflict. They would also have been aware of the atrocities that the Nazis and others had committed and been conscious of the full extent of human wickedness. It would have been easy to convince them of the necessity of Britain investing time, energy and money into the possibility of developing chemical and biological weapons. After all, other nastier and more unpredictable governments would.

We are not so easily persuaded today, as demonstrated by the response of people in the Outer Hebrides to a suggestion by the senior British politician Michael Gove (among others) during the Covid-19 crisis. He put forward the idea that the Scottish islands were perfect locations to develop strategies to end the lockdown, claiming there was 'scientific justification' for piloting measures such as contact tracing and to 'relax measures at a progressively greater rate' on some island communities before the rest of the UK.

The reaction towards his words was strong. Claiming – rightly! – that places like the Outer Hebrides had a larger percentage of older, vulnerable people among its population than most areas in the country, some pointed out that the islands had far too often been used for 'experimentation'. Its people were not to be employed as 'guinea pigs' in any such scheme. The choice of this language is interesting in the context of Operation Cauldron, but one wonders too if this feeling of distrust of authority and its ploys has also been engendered by other moments in the history of the islands: the initial failure to honour pledges of returning soldiers being given croftland, as promised before the First World War; the high percentage of men lost in that conflict; the cover-up and failure even to have a proper inquest after the *Iolaire* tragedy.[3] Operation Cauldron was just another chapter in this history of distrust and perceived betrayals. Its legacy could be seen in the way in which the Western Isles was for many years the most 'deviant political constituency' in the British Isles, the rural area with – in percentage terms – the smallest number of Conservative and Liberal voters in the country. It may also be a reason contributing to the current success of the SNP in the area.

The Covid-19 crisis has also produced its own interesting echoes of the events surrounding Operation Cauldron. Chief among them was an incident in August 2020 when – around the same time as a major outbreak in Aberdeen – a coronavirus cluster of five or so cases in Orkney was said to have been caused by the arrival of a fishing boat from Peterhead, its crew passing on the virus to a number of locals.

Another recent event that brought the circumstances of Operation Cauldron to mind was a Home Office discussion about the placement of asylum seekers who have arrived on these shores. Among the suggestions put forward was that those in that situation could be sent to island locations like Ascension and St Helena. The notion that offshore islands could be used as prisons or refugee camps has been mooted

---

[3]   See my book *As The Women Lay Dreaming* for some information about the circumstances of this.

previously. It is not only in the United States that the authorities have mentioned the possibility of employing a nearby 'Alcatraz' or 'Gannet Island' for these individuals. At the end of the fifteenth century, for instance, the island of Inchkeith in the Firth of Forth became a new home for those citizens of Edinburgh who were suffering from syphilis. Few survived the experience.

On a personal level, this book was inspired by much of my recent reading, including novels such as Patrick Hamilton's *Twenty Thousand Streets Under The Sky* and Olga Tokarczuk's *Drive Your Plow Over The Bones Of The Dead*, from which I 'borrowed' the notion of using some of William Blake's poetry in the text. Factual books that provided me with much of my information about biological and chemical weapons were Ken Alibek and Stephen Handelman's *Biohazard* and John Parker's *The Killing Factory*.

My information about Gibraltar came from a variety of sources. These included Nicholas Rankin's *Defending The Rock*, Paul Preston's *The Spanish Holocaust*, as well as *Little Wilson and Big God*, which is the first part of the autobiography of the writer Antony Burgess, who served there during part of World War Two. Most of all, however, my knowledge of Gibraltar's history is derived from my time there as the artistic representative from the Western Isles at the NatWest International Island Games in July 2019. I would like to thank Malcolm Burr and the Western Isles Council (Comhairle nan Eilean Siar) for their support with travel costs to and from Gibraltar after I spoke to them earlier that year about my ideas for a follow-up novel to *As The Women Lay Dreaming*. My accommodation there was – like a number of other artists from islands across the world – paid for by those involved in the NatWest International Island Games. Thanks to everyone who was involved in this. I would especially like to thank Alan John Perez, Shane Dalmedo, Davina Barbara and the many others whom I met there for their hard work and warm welcome. I particularly wish to express my gratitude to Ed Smith, Aaron Yeandle and Alan John Perez (once again) for their time accompanying me to the World War Two tunnels in Gibraltar. It would have been very lonely without your presence.

My knowledge of Tolsta goes back to my childhood and teenage years, when I used to visit relatives who came from that village. I now recognise one of them, the late George Morrison, who lived in Kinlochleven, as being a great visual storyteller, long before that term was invented. His sister, Ishbal Morrison, actually worked in the school canteen. It should be noted that neither Jessie nor Mairead are based on her. It was simply the case that this job – particularly at the time – would have provided these characters with an opportunity to learn Gaelic songs. I am grateful for the help that three natives of Tolsta – Catriona Macleod (or Murray), the musician Willie Campbell and my namesake Donald Murray – gave me in the creation of this novel. It should be pointed out that any mistakes in connection with this village's geography are, like any other errors, mine and mine alone. I would have liked to have obtained the opportunity to walk through Tolsta once again but circumstances in 2020 did not allow.

My knowledge of Gaelic music goes back a long time – to the days of the Ness Hall when I used to hear John 'Hoddan' Macdonald sing and the music of the late Murdo Macfarlane (and others) reverberate round the building's walls. My thanks to both Angus Campbell for allowing me to use Murdo's lyrics and to members of Hoddan's family for permitting me to use him as a character on the football field. (Apparently, even more than music, that was his greatest love.) Again, I would like to thank Catriona Murray for her book, *Le Mùirn*, which was very helpful in terms of the lyrics of Murdo Macfarlane. Shona Cormack's translations – found in that work – were the basis of my own. Her husband, Arthur, was also invaluable in this field, supplying me with the words of one Gaelic song that was on the edge of my thoughts. Arthur's remarkable memory for music has often proved invaluable when I'm in need! *Tapadh leibh uile.*

Finally, there is an abundance of people who have assisted me in the creation of this book to whom thanks are owed. Both Malcolm Macdonald and Kenny Macleod are terrific sources when it comes to island football – and more. I would also like to express my gratitude to my former classmate and erstwhile MP for the Western Isles, Calum Macdonald, for – like his predecessor, the late Donald Stewart MP in 1979 – asking questions about Operation Cauldron during his time in office. This whetted my curiosity about the incident and is probably one of the sources and inspirations for this book.

Others to thank include my former colleagues, in very different fields: Tom Maciver and Iain Morrison; Angus Murray; Eileen Scott; Catriona Murray; Liza Mulholland; Allan Macleod; Iain Mackenzie; Maria and Andrew Robertson; Iain Gordon Macdonald; Hugh Macinnes; Donald 'Ryno' Morrison; Rob Dunbar; Noreen Crighton; Liza Mulholland; the late Ian Broadfoot (historian of Inverness Caledonian Thistle football club); my classmate Allan George Macaskill; Christine

Davidson; Iain 'Costello' Maciver; Dolina Maclennan; Anna Maria Scaramuccia (whose family owned the Lido); those who informed me on Facebook about the kind of beers available in Stornoway in the Fifties, Donald Meek, Catriona Dunn (who was particularly helpful in correcting my Gaelic grammar), Catriona Morrison, Tom Clark; Iain Mackenzie, Roy Macintyre and the staff of Gairloch Museum who provided me with information about Aultbea in the early Forties.

My gratitude also goes to my editor, Craig Hillsley, who did so much remarkable work both in *As The Women Lay Dreaming* and this novel, the cover artist Andrew Forteath, and my publisher, Sara Hunt. It's great to be in their company.

Finally, there's Maggie. My love and thanks go especially to her.

Donald S Murray

The Author

Originally from the Isle of Lewis, Donald S Murray won the Paul Torday Memorial Award (2020) for his first novel and the Callum Macdonald Memorial Award at Scotland's National Book Awards. A writer, poet, and teacher, his work has also been nominated for the *Herald* Scottish Culture Awards, the Highland Book Prize, and the Author's Club First Novel Award. His critically acclaimed non-fiction brings to life the culture and nature of the Scottish islands, and he appears regularly on BBC Radio 4 and BBC Radio Scotland.

In the small hours of January 1st, 1919, the cruellest twist of fate changed at a stroke the lives of an entire community.

A deeply moving novel about passion constrained, coping with loss and a changing world, *As the Women Lay Dreaming* explores how a single event can so dramatically impact communities, individuals and, indeed, our very souls.

WINNER OF THE PAUL TORDAY MEMORIAL PRIZE

"A classic Bildungsroman." *Allan Massie, Scotsman*

"I loved this book." *Douglas Stuart, Booker Prize-winning novelist*

"Flawlessly written and cleverly structured … destined to be read for many generations to come." *Graeme Macrae Burnet*

"A book that's big with beauty, poetry and heart … full of memorable images and singing lines of prose." *Sarah Waters*

"A searing, poetic meditation on stoicism and loss." Mariella Frostrup, *Open Book*

9 781913 393007